The Secret of the Crooked Cat

Also in Armada
Alfred Hitchcock and The Three Investigators in

The Secret of Terror Castle
The Mystery of the Stuttering Parrot
The Mystery of the Whispering Mummy
The Mystery of the Green Ghost
The Mystery of the Vanishing Treasure
The Secret of Skeleton Island
The Mystery of the Fiery Eye
The Mystery of the Silver Spider
The Mystery of the Screaming Clock
The Mystery of the Moaning Cave
The Mystery of the Talking Skull
The Mystery of the Laughing Shadow
The Mystery of the Coughing Dragon
The Mystery of the Flaming Footprints
The Mystery of the Nervous Lion
The Mystery of the Singing Serpent
The Mystery of the Shrinking House

Alfred Hitchcock and
The Three Investigators

in

The Secret of the
Crooked Cat

Text by William Arden
Based on characters created by Robert Arthur

First published in the U.K. in 1971 by
William Collins Sons & Co. Ltd., London and Glasgow.
First published in Armada 1973 by
William Collins Sons & Co. Ltd., 14 St. James's Place,
London SW1A 1PF

Printed in Great Britain by
Love & Malcomson Ltd., Brighton Road,
Redhill, Surrey.

A Word from

Alfred Hitchcock

WELCOME, mystery lovers! It is my pleasure once again to introduce the trio of lads who call themselves The Three Investigators. "We Investigate Anything" is their motto—and so they do, whether invited to or not. That is why, presumably, they started snooping about an accident-prone carnival, poking their noses into other people's mysterious business, ferreting out the secret of a stuffed cat, eavesdropping—

But I am wrong to denigrate their youthful enthusiasm. They are good lads, if a trifle over-curious. In case you are meeting them for the first time, I should tell you that Jupiter Jones, the overweight leader of The Three Investigators, is known for his remarkable brain power. Pete Crenshaw is tall and muscular and excels at athletics. Bob Andrews, the smallest of the three, attends to research and keeps records for the group, but has the courage of a lion when danger threatens.

All three make their home in Rocky Beach, a small municipality in California a few miles from Hollywood. Their Headquarters is a mobile home trailer in The Jones Salvage Yard, a super junkyard owned by Jupiter's aunt and uncle.

If The Three Investigators had stopped to think that the mysterious crooked cat was leading them into their thirteenth case, they might have been less nosey. Bad luck attended them throughout—but I will say no more. I am sure you are anxious to dispense with this preview and proceed to the main feature.

ALFRED HITCHCOCK

1

Carnival!

ON AN AFTERNOON in early September, Jupiter Jones and Pete Crenshaw were busily working in Jupiter's workshop in The Jones Salvage Yard. To be honest, Jupiter was working while Pete watched, and it was Pete who first saw Uncle Titus Jones staggering up to them carrying two big wooden tubs.

"Boys," Uncle Titus announced as he plunked down the two tubs in front of them, "I have a job for you. I want these tubs painted in red, white and blue stripes!"

Pete gaped at the tubs. "Stripes on washtubs?"

"You mean right this minute, Uncle Titus?" Jupiter asked.

The stocky boy looked glumly at the array of tiny electronic parts on his workbench.

"Jupe's building a new thingumajig for The Three Investigators," Pete explained to Uncle Titus.

"A new invention, eh?" Uncle Titus said, momentarily distracted from his washtubs. "What is it, Pete?"

"Who knows? Gosh, you know Jupiter," Pete exclaimed. "I'm just the helper. Who tells me anything?"

Jupiter, the First Investigator of the boys' junior detective firm, liked to keep his inventions secret until he was sure that they would work. He hated to fail. He also hated to stop one of his projects before it was finished.

7

"Couldn't we paint the tubs later, Uncle Titus?" he now asked unhappily.

"No, they must be ready for tonight. Of course, if you boys are so busy, I could ask Hans or Konrad to paint them." Uncle Titus was referring to the big Bavarian brothers who helped in the yard. His eyes twinkled suddenly. "But then they'd deliver the tubs, too. That would be only fair."

Jupiter became alert. "Is there something special about who bought the tubs, Uncle Titus?"

"I know," Pete said. "It's a patriotic laundry!"

"Or holiday boats for midgets!" Jupiter chimed in.

Uncle Titus grinned. "What would you say if I said they were seats for a lion?"

"Oh, sure," Pete said with a laugh. "Every lion needs a red, white and blue easy chair."

Jupiter stopped laughing. A sudden light dawned in his eyes. "Of course! Turned upside down and painted, those tubs would be perfect as seats for a lion in a circus!"

"Wow! A circus!" Pete exclaimed. "Maybe they'd show us round if we deliver the tubs."

Uncle Titus chuckled at the effect of his news. "Well now, boys, it's not a real circus, just a carnival. But it does have performing shows as well as rides and games. It opened here in Rocky Beach last night. The lion trainer lost the pedestals for his trained lion in a fire or something. When he couldn't find any pedestals in town, he phoned us, and I thought of the tubs!"

Uncle Titus beamed happily. He always boasted that The Jones Salvage Yard had almost everything in its piles of junk, and nothing pleased him more than to have some seemingly useless item prove valuable to someone.

"A carnival," Jupiter pronounced, "is a most unique and fascinating organization with ancient origins."

8

"I guess you mean it's fun, Jupe," Pete said with a groan. The Second Investigator didn't always understand Jupiter's way of speaking. "Carson's Colossal Carnival! I remember now. I saw it being set up on that big piece of ground on the waterfront next to the old amusement park they closed down."

"Maybe we could go behind the scenes," Jupiter said.

"Then what are we waiting for, Jupe?" Pete cried. "I'll get the paint, you get the spray guns."

The boys went to work with a will, and half an hour later the tubs were painted. While they were drying, Jupiter and Pete went into their secret Headquarters to see how much money they had to spend at the carnival.

Headquarters was an old mobile home trailer, completely hidden behind mounds of junk in a remote corner of the yard. The boys could only enter by secret passages through the junk. By now everyone else had forgotten the trailer was there.

When the tubs were ready, Pete cycled to the Rocky Beach Public Library to tell Bob Andrews about the carnival. Bob, the Records and Research man of The three Investigators, worked part-time at the library during the summer. Bob was as much excited by the plans as Pete and Jupiter, and rushed home as soon as he was off duty. All three boys hurried through their dinners. By seven-thirty they were on their way, with the painted tubs balanced precariously on two of their bicycles.

While they were still some streets away, they could see the sagging towers and crumbling old roller coaster of the abandoned amusement park next to the carnival. The carnival itself was pitched on vacant ground beside the ocean. It wasn't yet open. Tents and wooden booths lined both sides of two wide pathways inside a temporary fence. Lights blazed in the early twilight, and the

9

music of the carousel played to entice the crowd. The empty Ferris wheel was already turning. Two clowns cavorted along one of the paths. Everyone was warming up for the opening.

The boys located the lion trainer's tent, emblazoned with a gaudy red banner that proclaimed: The Great Ivan and Rajah—The World's Greatest Performing Lion!! As they entered, a tall man in a bright blue uniform and gleaming black boots hurried towards them, his fierce moustache bristling.

"So, the tubs! Perfect! Give them to me!"

"The Jones Salvage Yard has what you want," Jupiter said, announcing Uncle Titus's slogan for the yard.

The Great Ivan laughed. "That sounds like one of our barkers, young man."

"What's a barker, sir?" Pete asked.

"Well, son, suppose you try to guess," The Great Ivan said.

"I'll bet Jupe knows," Bob declared.

Both Bob and Pete had learned that Jupiter usually knew a little about everything, and the stocky leader of the trio wasn't bashful about telling what he knew.

"A barker," Jupiter now pronounced, "is a man who stands outside a circus or carnival sideshow and tells people how exciting it is inside. You could say it was an ancient form of advertising."

"Very good, young man," The Great Ivan said. "Sometimes we call them 'spielers' or 'pitchmen', and sometimes they lie, but not the good ones. My barker, for instance, doesn't tell people that Rajah is a ferocious lion, he just tells them some of what Rajah can do. Did you ever see a lion on a trapeze?"

"Wow! Can Rajah ride on a trapeze?" Pete exclaimed.

"He can," The Great Ivan boasted. "First show in

an hour, boys. Come as my guests. Perhaps you can touch Rajah even."

"We'll be here, sir!" Bob promised eagerly.

Outside, the carnival had just opened, and the barkers were announcing the attractions to the few early arrivals. The boys rode on the Ferris wheel and tried the carousel twice. They vied for the brass ring, but only Pete got one. They watched the antics of one small, fat clown for a time, then went towards the game booths where prizes could be won for dart throwing, ring tossing and rifle shooting.

"The games must be faked, fellows," Bob observed after he had watched for a time. "They look too easy."

"No," Jupiter explained, "it's simply that they're much more difficult than they seem. A matter of mathematics and physics, Records. The odds—"

The rest of Jupiter's explanation was drowned out by a sudden shouting in front of them.

"You're a cheat! Give me that prize!"

Ahead of them was a tall, older man in a slouch hat. He had a thick, bushy moustache and wore dark glasses, even though it was almost dark. He was shouting at the blond boy who operated the shooting gallery. Suddenly he grabbed a stuffed animal from the boy's hands and ran straight towards The Three Investigators.

The blond boy shouted, "Stop him! Thief! Guards!"

2

Stop Thief!

"Look out!" Pete cried.

His warning came too late. The running man, looking behind him for pursuit, ran full tilt into Jupiter. They both fell in a tangle of arms and legs.

"Ooooooff!" Jupiter grunted.

Two carnival guards ran up as the few early visitors scattered.

"You! Stay right there!" one of the guards shouted to the moustached thief in dark glasses.

The thief leaped up first, stuck his stolen prize under one arm, and grabbed Jupiter. A wicked knife gleaming in his free hand.

"Don't come near me," he rasped menacingly, and awkwardly began to drag Jupiter towards the exit from the carnival.

Bob and Pete could only watch in horror. The two carnival guards tried to circle round behind. The thief saw them. He was momentarily distracted, and Jupiter seized the chance to try to break loose and run. With an oath, the thief whirled back to face Jupiter. Off balance, the stuffed animal still held awkwardly under his arm, he stumbled and his hand holding the knife struck Jupiter's shoulder. The knife flew from his grasp.

In a flash the thief saw that he could not retrieve his knife in time. He released Jupiter, pushed him sprawling towards the guards, and ran off through the exit with the stolen prize.

Suddenly Jupiter was sent sprawling . . .

Jupiter staggered up again, crying out, "After him!"

The boys raced after the fleeing thief, followed by the two carnival guards. The moustached man ran towards the ocean and disappeared behind a jutting corner of the high wooden fence that surrounded the abandoned amusement park. The guards caught up with the boys.

"All right, boys," a guard said. "We'll deal with him."

"It's a dead end round that corner," Pete panted. "The fence goes down to the water. He's trapped!"

"Stay here then," the second guard ordered the boys.

The two guards, their pistols out, went cautiously round the corner of the fence. The boys waited. There was a long silence after the two guards had vanished. Jupiter became impatient.

"Something must be wrong," the First Investigator said. "Come on, fellows."

Cautiously, Jupiter led them round the corner of the high fence. They stopped in their tracks. The two guards stood there alone. The moustached old thief was gone!

"No one was here," one guard said.

Stunned, the boys looked round the small grassy area. The high fence was on the right, the deep water of the ocean on the left. At the far end the fence made a sharp angle all the way down to the ocean. A spiked iron extension of the fence reached out over the water. There was no way out except the way they had come in!

"You boys must have made a mistake," the second guard said.

"Maybe he swam away," Bob suggested.

"No time, son. We'd have seen him in the water," the first guard said. "He must have fooled you."

"No, I saw him run right in here," Jupiter insisted stubbornly.

Pete had been staring all round. Now the tall Second Investigator exclaimed, "Look!"

He bent and picked up a large object from the shadows. It was the stuffed animal the moustached man had stolen. Pete held it up triumphantly.

"He was here, all right," Pete declared.

"He must have dropped it getting out of here," Bob said. His face was puzzled as he looked all round the small, closed-in-area. "But how did he get out?"

"There must be some way through that fence," the first guard said.

"A hole or a door," said the second guard.

"Maybe a tunnel under the fence," Pete suggested.

They all examined the fence for the entire length of the hidden area and found nothing.

"No," Jupiter observed. "This part of the fence seems to be in good repair, and there isn't any way under it, either."

"Then he must have had wings!" one guard declared. "That's the only way out of here except past us as we came in."

"That fence is twelve feet high or more," the other guard said, "and there's nothing to get hold of. No one could climb over it."

Jupiter was thoughtful as they all stared up at the fence. "If he didn't swim, or dig, or fly, logically there is only one possibility—he went over the fence.'

"That's crazy," a guard insisted.

"Gosh, First," Pete said, "how could anyone climb that fence without help? There's nothing to stand on."

Bob said, "He couldn't have climbed it, Jupe."

"No, it wouldn't seem so," Jupiter said, "but there just isn't any other logical explanation, so he must have. When everything else is ruled out, what is left must be true, even if it looks impossible."

15

"Well, however he did it, he's gone," one guard said. "We'd better get back to our posts. We'll take that prize back to the shooting gallery."

The guard reached his hand out for the stuffed animal Pete was still holding. Jupiter, who was continuing to stare upward at the solid fence, now turned to the guard.

'We'd like to return the prize, if that's all right with you,' the First Investigator said. "We were about to attempt to win a prize at the shooting gallery anyway."

"Okay," the guard agreed. "You take it back. That'll save us some time. We'll have to report that thief to the police."

After the guards had left, while the boys were walking back to the carnival, Pete said, "I didn't know we were going to try the shooting gallery, First."

"Perhaps we weren't," Jupiter acknowledged, "but I'm interested to know just why that man attacked the boy at the gallery and stole this prize."

He pointed at the stuffed animal in Pete's hands, and the boys really looked at it for the first time. Pete's eyes almost popped in excitement as he examined the prize he held.

"Wow! It's a beaut, isn't it?"

It was a stuffed cat almost three feet long, striped red and black. Its legs were all twisted, and the body was crooked like a Z. Its mouth was open showing sharp, white teeth, and one ear drooped sharply down. There was only one wild red eye, and a jewelled red collar. It was the wildest, most crooked-looking cat they had ever seen.

"It certainly is striking," Jupiter agreed. "But I wonder why that man wanted it so much?"

"Maybe he collects stuffed animals," Bob suggested. "My Dad says collectors'll do anything to get what they want."

"He collects stuffed cats?" Peter scoffed. "From a carnival? That's crazy, Records. How much could it be worth?"

"Well," Jupited considered, "it does sound foolish, but collectors are strange people sometimes. There are rich men who buy stolen paintings even though they have to hide them. It's what they call an obsession, and collectors with obsessions commit desperate acts. But I don't think our thief is really a collector. More likely he's one of those people who can't bear to lose at anything. Or perhaps he became violent because he felt he'd won and been cheated."

"I guess even we might get mad if we'd been cheated," Pete agreed, "but we wouldn't get violent about it."

They reached the shooting gallery, and the blond boy behind the counter greeted them eagerly.

"You got my cat back! Did they catch that old man?"

"He got away," Pete said, "but he dropped the cat."

Pete handed the crooked cat to the boy.

"I hope the police catch him," the boy said angrily. "He only knocked down three of the five ducks! A real bad loser. Gosh, you fellows really chased him." The boy grinned. "I'm Andy Carson. I work this booth. Are you fellows with it?"

Bob blinked. "Are we what, Andy?"

"He means," the always ready Jupiter explained, "are we carnival people, from some other carnival. No, Andy, we lived in Rocky Beach. I'm Jupiter Jones, and they're Bob Andrews and Pete Crenshaw."

"Glad to meet you, fellows," Andy said, and added proudly, "I'm with it. A full operator, not just a punk or a roughneck."

"Huh?" Pete said.

"A 'punk'," Jupiter interpreted for the others, "is an apprentice member of the carnival, and a 'roughneck' is a manual workman. Andy means he's just like a proper adult performer in the carnival. That's pretty unusual, isn't it, Andy?"

"Well," Andy said, a little sheepishly, "my Dad owns the show. But he says I could work any carnival now anyway. Say, would you fellows like to try winning a prize?"

"I'd like to win that crooked cat!" Pete exclaimed.

"We could make it our mascot," Bob said.

"A symbol of our work," Jupiter agreed. "Go on, Pete, try."

Andy Carson grinned. "You have to hit five targets in five shots to win the crooked cat. It's a first prize. It's not easy, but it can be done. I've given out four cats so far."

"I'll win the fifth," Pete declared, and reached for one of the rifles chained to the gallery counter.

Suddenly, Andy jumped at Pete, his hand out.

"Wait," he cried.

3

A Dangerous Moment

"WHAT IS IT, ANDY?" Peter asked, alert.

Andy grinned and put a straw hat on his head. "Not so fast, young man. Your eagerness to test your skill is admirable, yes it is, but first it is necessary to cross my palm with silver, coin of the realm, legal currency to the amount of twenty-five cents, the fourth part of a dollar. A mere trifle for five big shots. Step up, my boy, everybody wins. Show your steady hand and keen eye. Give the man room, please. Five little hits wins the big prize, the one-and-only amazing crooked cat!"

The boys laughed, and Pete dug into his pocket for a quarter.

"Gosh," Bob said, "do you always talk like that, Andy?"

Andy beamed. "My Dad says I've got carnival in my blood. He says I'm a natural spieler."

"You sure are," Bob said. "Can you teach us?"

"Ah, my boy," Andy intoned, his face solemn, "it is first necessary to study long years with the Great Lama of Nepal. At the appropriate moment, after that, some small instruction could be made available for a modest fee. Only a selected few, of course, can be permitted the honour—"

Grinning, the boys listened as Andy spiled on in a fantastic performance of flowery words. Andy, too, grinned as he talked, pleased with his verbal ability.

"But now," he concluded with a flourish, "stand aside, give the young nimrod room to show his skill. Fire at will, Pete!"

Pete nodded and picked up one of the rifles. After a moment of studying the targets, he took quick aim at the clanking procession of mechanical ducks and shot down three in a row. Andy clapped his hands.

"Good, Pete! Careful now, only two more!"

Pete fired again, hitting a fourth duck.

'One more! Steady," Andy warned. "Easy now. Careful!"

Andy winked at Bob and Jupiter. They understood: Andy's warnings and encouragements were actually carnival tricks to make Pete more nervous with each shot, increasing his chances of a miss. But Pete didn't fluster once he was in action. He aimed once more, fired, and knocked down the fifth duck.

"I won!" he cried.

"Bravo, Pete," Andy said, and handed the dazzling crooked cat to the Second Investigator. "You're a good shot. That's my last crooked cat. I'll have to use a different first prize until I get more. I think I have some moon globes."

Jupiter's eyes gleamed. "A moon globe? They only just came out, Andy. Could we win one of those, too?"

"Try your luck, my boy," Andy said, assuming his barker's voice again. "A steady hand and keen eye! Five shots."

While Pete and Bob laughed, Jupiter picked up a rifle and paid Andy a quarter. He took good aim and hit two ducks. But he missed the next three.

"Let me try, Jupe," Bob said.

The smallest of the three boys paid Andy a quarter and aimed at a swinging gong. He fared no better than Jupiter, hitting the gong only twice. After that, Pete tried again, hoping to win the moon globe for Jupiter, but this time even he failed.

"A mere mischance," Andy said. "Next time a successful result is assured. One more twenty-five cent piece!"

Pete shook his head. "I'd better quit while I'm even, I guess. At least I won the cat."

They all laughed at that, and other customers began to step up to the booth. The carnival had become more crowded. Andy went into his full spiel while the boys watched. Then Andy realized that he was telling the people they could win a moon globe and he didn't have any on display.

"Jupiter, you get behind the counter and watch the booth while I go and get some globes. Pete and Bob can help me carry some," Andy said.

"Sure, Andy," Bob agreed. "Go on, Jupe."

Jupiter needed no urging. He went behind the booth counter at once and began trying to spiel like Andy. The growing crowd seemed to enjoy the chunky boy's performance, and Jupiter beamed with pleasure.

Andy led Bob and Pete behind the booth where a small

baggage trailer stood in the dimmer light out of the main carnival area.

"I park it close where I can watch it from the booth," Andy explained. "People are always trying to steal from carnivals."

He unlocked the lid of the trailer and began to take out small globes that were perfect models of the moon. He removed six globes, relocked the trailer, and turned to hand two globes to Bob.

"Bob, you—" Andy began, and then stopped. His eyes widened as he looked past Pete towards the next booth. His voice came low. "Fellows, don't move. Stand still."

Bob frowned. "No more carnival tricks, Andy, we—"

"No," Andy whispered, his voice tense and scared, yet steady. "Turn round slowly, fellows. Don't run, and don't make any sudden moves. It's Rajah!"

The boys stared at Andy, and Pete gulped. Slowly, they turned round. There was a dim, grassy space behind the next booth, out of sight from the main alley. In that space, not twenty feet from the boys, crouched a large, black-maned lion!

4

Peter Shows His Courage

"Back slowly towards the booth," Andy instructed softly. "Rajah isn't a dangerous lion, he's too well-trained, but he could become frightened and panic. In the booth we'll be safe, and there's a telephone. I can call for help."

No one else had yet seen the escaped lion where it

crouched behind the next booth. Its yellow eyes glinted as it watched the boys, and its mouth opened wide to show enormous yellow teeth. Its black-tufted tail twitched.

"But if we go to the booth," Pete said, his voice shaky, "the lion could get out into the main alley with the crowd, Andy."

"I know, and the lights and people could scare him," Andy agreed, "but we have to call Ivan for help!"

Pete didn't take his eyes off the menacing lion.

"You . . . you and Bob go to the booth and call Ivan," he said. "I . . . I've worked with my Dad with animals he used in his movies. It could be a lot more dangerous if we all try to leave."

"Pete!" Bob cried, scared.

The lion growled softly at the sound of Bob's voice.

"Go on, hurry, fellows," Pete insisted in a whisper.

The tall boy hadn't moved. He stood and stared straight at the crouched lion. Bob and Andy backed towards the booth. The lion moved a long step, its eyes watching Bob and Andy. It was obviously nervous and confused by being out of its cage. Pete spoke quietly but firmly, and the lion looked at him.

"Stop, Rajah," Pete said. "Lie down, Rajah."

His voice was soft but strong, confident. The lion stopped. It looked at Pete with wary yellow eyes.

"Quiet, Rajah," Pete said. "Good, Rajah."

With its tail flicking slowly, the lion watched Pete as if it knew its name and was puzzled by hearing it from a strange boy. Pete didn't look behind him towards Andy's booth. He watched only the big lion.

"Lie down, Rajah. Down, Rajah!"

Pete's voice rose firmly on the last command.

"Down, Rajah!"

The lion whipped its tail, looked round, and lay down heavily on the grass. With its head up, it watched Pete like a big cat about to purr.

"Good, Rajah," Pete said.

Suddenly Pete heard people behind him, and The Great Ivan strode past him towards Rajah. The lion trainer carried only a stick and a long chain. He went straight up to the lion and began to talk softly but firmly, just as Pete had. Moments later he had the chain attached to a collar hidden in Rajah's great mane and was leading the obedient lion back behind the booths towards his cage.

Pete gulped and went white. "Gosh!" he said.

Bob, Jupiter, and Andy ran up to him.

"Pete, that was great!" Andy cried.

"You were magnificent, Second!" Jupiter declared. "No one even knew Rajah was loose. You certainly prevented a panic!"

"I was too scared even to breathe!" Bob added.

Pete blushed under their praises. Before he could answer, they all saw The Great Ivan striding back towards them. The trainer's face was pale, and he grasped Pete's shoulder in an iron grip of approval.

"That was very brave, young man. You showed both courage and skill," The Great Ivan said. "Rajah is trained, and really tame. He wouldn't harm anyone. But if the crowd had seen him loose, they could have panicked, and that would have scared Rajah. Someone could have been hurt."

Pete grinned with embarrassment. "I knew he was trained, sir, and Andy said he wasn't dangerous. My Dad taught me a lot about handling trained wild animals."

The Great Ivan nodded. "Your Dad taught you well. Rajah needed to hear a firm, commanding voice. I owe you a great debt. I don't know how he got out! The cage was open." Then the lion trainer grinned. "Now, what do you boys say to watching Rajah and me from right beside my show cage, eh?"

"Can we, sir?" Pete exclaimed.

"You certainly can. Come to the tent in a few minutes. I have to be sure Rajah is ready for his show."

The Great Ivan returned to his tent. The boys stayed with Andy Carson for a few moments as the carnival boy went back to work. People crowded round the shooting gallery now, and Andy became very busy.

The boys started for the lion tent, stopping on the way to watch the antics of the two clowns who were out among the crowd. The small, fat clown whom they had watched earlier had been joined by his tall, sad-faced companion. The tall clown had a white-painted, dirty face with a thin red nose. He was dressed as a tramp, with enormous baggy trousers tied at the bottom. The fat little clown's nose lighted up like neon at appropriate moments.

The little clown did a series of acrobatic tricks, strutting like a bantam peacock after each one. The tall clown watched mournfully and tried to do the same tricks, but failed every time. His face grew sadder and sadder, and the crowd roared with laughter at him. Finally, the fat little clown missed a handstand and sprawled flat. The sad clown smiled at last. The boys applauded the clowns.

"A very good act," Jupiter declared. "Did you see how it all built up to the sad clown finally smiling? People enjoy that, the sad one having a moment of victory. When I was in the movies I worked with clowns. These are very good."

People were sometimes surprised by Jupiter's knowledge of the movies and TV. They forgot that the First Investigator had once been a child performer under the name of Baby Fatso. It was a name Jupiter didn't like to be reminded of now, but he liked to display his knowledge of show business.

When the clown act was over, the boys hurried on to the lion tent. The show cage was in the outer half of the tent in front of a canvas partition. A barred ramp came down into the show cage from behind the partition. The

24

two striped tubs Pete and Jupiter had painted stood inside the show cage and a trapeze swung from the top.

Just as the boys entered the tent The Great Ivan stepped out from behind the canvas divider. He bowed to them and entered the show cage. He gave a signal, and Rajah came down the barred ramp into the cage roaring like the wildest beast on earth! He ran round the cage snarling, and clawed towards The Great Ivan.

The boys smiled. They were aware that Rajah's ferocious manner was an act the same as that of any trained performer. Their eyes widened with admiration as The Great Ivan began to put Rajah through jumps, rolls, leaps, dance steps, somersaults, and finally, a great leap to the swinging trapeze!

The audience applauded lustily.

"Wow!" Pete said. "All I did was make him lie down!"

"Isn't it great, Jupe!" Bob cried. "Jupe?"

The First Investigator was no longer with them. They finally spotted him behind the cage where The Great Ivan was performing an encore with Rajah. Jupiter was motioning for them to come over.

"What's up, First?" Bob wanted to know.

Jupiter didn't answer, but motioned them both through the canvas partition into the rear half of the tent. A barred trailer stood in the empty rear section. It was, clearly, where Rajah lived when he wasn't in the show cage. The barred ramp led from it through the partition into the show cage.

Jupiter pointed to a large padlock on the door of the trailer cage.

"That lock's been tampered with, fellows," the First Investigator said grimly. "Someone let Rajah loose!"

5

A Menacing Shadow

"THE GREAT IVAN is a skilled trainer," Jupiter went on, "and he treats Rajah like a pet. I began to wonder how anyone could have left Rajah's cage open without Ivan noticing. So I came back here to look at the trailer cage. Look at this lock."

Jupiter held the big padlock. "See those deep scratches all around the keyhole? The steel shines in the scratches. This lock has been picked, and not long ago!"

"Are you sure, Jupe?" Bob asked uneasily.

Jupiter nodded. "Remember that book we have at Headquarters? The one about evidence and criminal methods? Well, those marks are exactly like pictures in that book of picklock marks!"

"Gosh," Pete said, "who would let a lion loose?"

As The Three Investigators thought about that, there was a burst of applause from the show section of the tent. An iron cage clanged, and Rajah came stalking proudly up the barred ramp into the trailer cage. The boys all stared at the big lion.

"It has to be someone crazy, First," Bob decided.

Jupiter's bright eyes were fixed on the lion in its cage. "Crazy and full of hate for people, perhaps, Records. But not necessarily. Maybe there was a definite reason, a motive."

"Gosh, Jupe, like what?" Pete asked.

"Well, to scare customers and harm the carnival, for one," Jupiter said. "Or to be a hero by recapturing

Rajah. Or maybe to hide some other action, to distract everyone."

"Nothing else happened, Jupe, did it?" Pete objected.

"And nobody tried to recapture Rajah until The Great Ivan came when Andy called him," Bob pointed out.

"I think Pete just acted too fast," Jupiter decided. "If there was some plan, Pete stopped it by stopping Rajah."

"But, gee, First," Bob said, "if someone only wanted to hurt the carnival, that's a risky way of doing it."

"I don't know," Jupiter mused. "Even Andy knew that Rajah wasn't really dangerous. The whole carnival seems to know that Rajah is well-trained and easily controlled."

"You think it was someone in the carnival?" Bob wondered.

Jupiter nodded. "Yes, I do. To get from his trailer cage to where Pete stopped him, Rajah almost had to be led."

"Gosh, First, it could be anyone—except The Great Ivan," Pete decided. "He wouldn't have had to pick his own lock."

"Not unless he wanted to fool people," Jupiter said. He thought a moment. "It's odd that Ivan didn't miss Rajah sooner."

Bob and Pete said nothing more for a time. Jupiter frowned.

"The trouble is," the First Investigator said, "that we don't know enough even to guess at who or why—yet."

"Yet?" Pete said. "You mean we're going to—"

"Investigate!" Bob broke in eagerly. "A job for The Three Investigators!"

"Yes, I think—" Jupiter began, and then stopped. Suddenly he put his finger to his lips and nodded towards the rear wall of the tent. Bob and Pete turned to look.

A giant shadow was outlined against the tent wall. The shadow of a man who seemed to have no clothes on! They could see massive shoulders, and the shadow of a shaggy head that was bent close to the tent, as if listening.

"Outside, fellows," Jupiter whispered.

There was no way out of the rear of the lion tent, so they slipped through the show section and out the front. They hurried round the corner of the tent, being as quiet as they could be, and at the rear peered cautiously round. No one was there.

"He must have heard us," Bob whispered.

There was a heavy step behind them.

"So there you are!" a deep voice said almost in their ears. "What are you boys doing back here?"

The boys jumped a foot, and Pete gulped as they turned and saw a big man looking down at them from dark eyes. He carried a long sledge hammer in his hands.

"W-w-we only—" Pete stammered.

At that moment Andy Carson appeared behind the big man. The carnival boy's eyes lighted up when he saw The Three Investigators.

"Hi, fellows," he said. "It looks like my Dad found you."

Pete gulped. "Your Dad?"

"That's right, boys." The big man smiled and rested his sledge hammer on the ground. "I've been looking for you to thank you on behalf of the whole carnival for keeping Rajah calm. I was off helping the roughnecks, so Andy couldn't find me at once."

Andy broke in, "My Dad wants to give you some reward. Something more from the carnival than that crooked cat you won."

"My cat!" Pete cried suddenly, and looked round. "I don't have it any more!"

"Cat?" Mr Carson said, puzzled.

"One of the first prizes from my gallery, Dad," Andy explained. "Pete won it."

"Maybe it's in the lion tent, Pete," Bob suggested.

But the crooked cat wasn't anywhere in the lion tent,

28

and they all went back to the shooting gallery. The cat wasn't anywhere in or around the gallery, or where Pete had calmed Rajah.

"I had it just before we saw Rajah," Pete said unhappily. "I must have dropped it, and someone picked it up."

Jupiter, who had been silently fuming with impatience ever since they had started to look for the crooked cat, now burst out, "I'm sure Andy can get you another, Pete. Mr Carson, when we—"

But Andy said, "Gee, I can't get Pete another cat. That was my last, remember? I had five, and gave them all out."

"I'm sure we can find something better," Mr Carson said.

Jupiter could contain himself no longer. He blurted out, "Is there trouble in your carnival, Mr Carson?"

"Trouble?" Mr Carson repeated, his deep, dark eyes on the First Investigator. "What makes you ask that?"

"Before you found us, sir, we observed a man watching us, or listening to us, at Rajah's tent."

"Watching you?" Mr Carson frowned, and then laughed. "No, you must be mistaken. Your imagination was probably working overtime after Rajah."

"That is possible," Jupiter admitted somewhat stiffly, "but we didn't imagine what we had discovered just before we saw that man listening. Rajah did not escape, he was let loose!"

Mr Carson watched them. "Come to my truck, boys."

The trucks, trailers and cars of the carnival people were parked in a field next to the show. Mr Carson and Andy lived in a truck with a trailer hookup on the rear. Inside were two bunks, chairs, a desk covered with business papers, a small safe, and a big wicker basket filled with damaged prizes—torn stuffed dogs, a dirty stuffed cat, broken dolls.

29

"I fix all the broken prizes," Andy said proudly.

Mr Carson was serious. "Sit down, boys, and tell me."

He listened intently as Jupiter described what they had found at Rajah's cage. "I've studied lock-picking, sir, and I recognized the marks. We're really experienced detectives."

Jupiter handed Mr Carson the boys' card:

THE THREE INVESTIGATORS

"We Investigate Anything"

? ? ?

First Investigator – JUPITER JONES
Second Investigator – PETER CRENSHAW
Records and Research – BOB ANDREWS

Mr Carson smiled. "An interesting hobby, boys, but—"

"Our works is more than a hobby, sir," Jupiter said proudly. "The Rocky Beach Police attest to our seriousness."

He presented the second card the boys carried:

This certifies that the bearer is a Volunteer Junior Assistant Deputy co-operating with the police force of Rocky Beach. Any assistance given him will be appreciated.

(Signed) Samuel Reynolds
Chief of Police

"I apologize, boys," Mr Carson smiled. "The Chief's statement seems to indicate you are real detectives. Still, you're mistaken this time."

"Jupe's never mistaken, sir," Bob declared.

"Come now, Bob. I'm sure that Jupiter is an amazing young man, but everyone can be mistaken."

"But, Dad!" Andy broke in, "what about—"

Mr Carson stood up. "That's enough, Andy! No more, you hear? Jupiter is mistaken. But the boys did us a service, and here are three free passes for everything at the carnival." He handed them to the boys. "Is that a good reward, boys?"

"That is very generous, sir," Jupiter acknowledged.

"Oh, no!" Bob cried. "Look, the door!"

On the drawn blind of the rear door they all saw a massive shadow with wild hair, beard, and enormous shoulder muscles.

"That's the shadow!" Pete hissed.

Mr Carson walked quickly to the door, opened it, and then turned to the boys smiling. A man entered, and the boys gaped at him. He was only normally tall, but his bare shoulders bulged with muscles. He wore only black-and-gold tights, which clung to his powerful legs like skin, and tight, gleaming leather boots. His black hair and beard stood out wild and thick.

"This," Mr Carson said, smiling, "is Khan, our strong man. One of your mysteries is explained, boys. Khan, like all of us, has more than one job. He's in charge of our security. I'd guess he saw you slipping round and decided to check on you."

"That is correct," Khan said in a deep, serious voice.

Mr Carson nodded. "There you are then, boys. Now I have business with Khan, and Andy must go back to his booth. You go and have fun. Remember, it's all free."

"Thank you, sir," Jupiter said quietly. He motioned to Bob and Pete. Outside the truck, Jupiter walked ahead until they were behind a trailer, out of sight of the truck. Then he suddenly stopped, ducked down, and peered back.

"What are you doing, Jupe?" Bob asked.

"I'm sure something is wrong in this carnival, Records," the First Investigator said. "That Khan has something on his mind. He didn't look much like a guard when he was listening to us. And I'm sure Andy would have told us something if his father hadn't stopped him. Let's get close to that window and listen."

"Wait!" Pete said quickly.

Andy Carson came out of the truck and hurried away towards his shooting gallery. The boys slipped up to the window.

Khan's deep voice was saying, ". . . now Rajah escapes. What next, Carson? Maybe we won't be paid at all."

"You'll all be paid next week, Khan," Mr Carson said.

Khan said, "You know how superstitious carnival people are. The show is unlucky. There will be more trouble."

"Now, Khan, listen to me. You—"

There was a step inside, and the window banged shut above the boys' heads. They heard no more and hurried away.

"Gosh, there *is* trouble," Pete exclaimed, "but what can we do if Mr Carson won't even talk about it?"

Jupiter was thoughtful. "He won't let Andy talk, either, but we have passes, and we can watch. Tomorrow, Bob can check the newspapers at the library for any stories of trouble at the carnival in other towns. Tomorrow, we'll meet and see what we can decide."

"What are you going to do, First?" Bob asked.

"I think," Jupiter said ominously, "I shall spend the rest of the night in search of the necessary knowledge."

6

Andy Is Amazed

PETE slept badly that night, trying to think of ways to make Mr Carson let the boys investigate. By morning he still had no ideas and was eager to find out if the other Investigators had thought of something. He hurried down to breakfast and found his father was up ahead of him.

"Gosh, you're up early, Dad," Pete said.

"A hurry call from Alfred Hitchcock," Mr Crenshaw explained. "Some special work on our new picture. Unfortunately, Pete, I promised your mother I'd clean out the basement today. I'm afraid you're elected to do it for me."

Pete groaned inwardly and said, "Sure, Dad. I'll do it."

That was why Pete didn't pedal his bike up to the Jones Salvage Yard until after lunch. In the yard he made his way to a long section of corrugated pipe that seemed to vanish into the mounds of junk. This was Tunnel Two, the main entrance to Headquarters. Pete crawled into the pipe and emerged up through the trap door into the trailer. Jupiter was there.

"Have you thought of a way to get Mr Carson to let us help?" the First Investigator asked promptly.

"No," Pete sighed. "I can't think of anything."

"Neither can I," Jupiter admitted glumly. "I guess we don't have a chance unless Bob finds something to help us at the library. I've been watching for him."

Jupiter was standing at the See-All, and now he peered into the eyepiece again. The See-All was a crude but efficient periscope Jupiter had built to remedy the one

33

disadvantage of Headquarters—they couldn't see out. The See-All stuck up above the junk that hid the trailer, looking like a piece of ordinary pipe, and the boys could see most of the salvage yard.

"There he is now!" Jupiter cried.

Moments later, Bob came up through the trap door waving a notebook and looking excited.

"You found troubles at the carnival?" Pete exclaimed.

Bob beamed. "It took all morning, but I got it! The carnival isn't very important, so I had to read most of the small-town newspapers."

"What did you find, Records?" Jupiter asked impatiently.

Bob opened his notebook. "Three weeks ago the carnival lost its pony ride in Ventura. Three of the ponies died of food poisoning. Then, three days ago there was a fire when they were just north in San Mateo. Three tents were burned: the fire eater's tent, the lion tent, and part of the shooting gallery. They were lucky to stop it."

"The lion tent?" Pete exclaimed. "That makes trouble there twice."

"It could be coincidence," Jupiter said. "We must never jump to conclusions. But it would be interesting to know if the pony ride was also located in the same carnival area."

"The papers didn't say, First," Bob said.

"No," Jupiter said thoughtfully. "Both so-called accidents could have been much worse. The carnival was lucky, unless—" Jupiter did not finish that thought. "I assumed that those two other accidents were all you found, Records?'

"How did you know that, Jupe?" Bob asked, puzzled.

"Last night we heard Khan mention superstition," Jupiter reminded them. "After I got home I talked to Uncle Titus and read some of his books—you remember Uncle Ttitus worked in a circus. One of the oldest carnival superstitions is that accidents happen in threes. So Rajah's escape was the third!"

"Gosh, do they still believe that?" Pete asked.

"Carnival people tend to live apart, Second, and hold to old beliefs," Jupiter explained. "But I did more than read carnival history last night. Uncle Titus told me of a book that lists all circus and carnival performers. I called the reference room of the Los Angeles library this morning. There is no listing for a strong man named Khan!"

"Khan's a fake?" Pete exclaimed.

"It could be he hasn't performed recently," Jupiter admitted. "Or he could be from out of the country. But there is something suspicious about Khan." His eyes gleamed. "And I've got an idea of how to get us involved with the carnival. We won't convince Mr Carson right away, but I think if we get Andy here we can convince him by following my plan."

"What plan is that, Jupe?" Pete asked.

Jupiter began to explain his plan, and after a few minutes both of the other boys were grinning and nodding.

A short while later Pete was again watching the salvage yard through the See-All. "Here he comes, fellows!"

When the blond carnival boy came up to the workshop outside Headquarters, Pete was waiting for him.

"What's up, Pete?" Andy asked.

"We thought you might like to see our secret Headquarters, and how we work," Pete said. "Come on."

He led the carnival boy into Tunnel Two and up through the trap door into the trailer.

"Jiminy! What a neat place!" Andy cried.

He stared wide-eyed at the microscope, telephone, periscope, walkie-talkies on the wall, filing cabinets, metal detector, shelves of books and trophies, and all the other equipment the boys had arranged so that Andy couldn't

35

miss it. He looked at Bob and Jupiter, who seemed to be hard at work. Neither of them even glanced up. Jupiter was peering through magnifying goggles at a lock and a book. Bob was studying something under a lighted glass screen.

Pete said in a low voice, "We know there's something wrong at your carnival, Andy. We're investigating the details."

"But you can't," Andy said. "You don't know."

"Science and our training will tell us what you won't, Andy," Pete declared, sounding as pompous as Jupiter.

Suddenly Jupiter stood up. "A professional criminal released Rajah, fellows," he announced as if unaware that Andy was in the room. "There is no doubt. The indentations on the exterior face of the lock are proximate patterns of a type-seven pick-lock! The purpose was certainly to cause trouble."

Andy stood and blinked at the stream of words he only half understood. Before he could gather his wits, Bob started talking.

"It's certain, now, that three weeks ago the deaths of three ponies caused the pony ride to be abandoned," the Records and Research man of the trio stated. "Then a fire destroyed three tents and part of the shooting gallery. This has caused financial loss, and Mr Carson has been unable to pay wages."

Still acting as if he didn't know Andy was present, Jupiter nodded and asked. "What do we know about the performers?"

"The strong man, Khan," Bob announced, "has no previous record of work in carnivals. Possibly he is an impostor."

Through this whole big act, Andy's mouth had dropped lower and lower. Now he could contain himself no longer.

36

Through goggles he was peering at a lock . . .

"Who told you all that?" he blurted out.

Both Bob and Jupiter turned as if amazed to find Andy in the room with them. Jupiter looked his most innocent.

"Andy, I didn't know you were here," he said.

"Someone had to tell you all that!" Andy said hotly.

"No, Andy," Jupiter shook his head. "We're investigators, and we simply found out. Do I understand we're correct?"

Andy nodded. "All of it, even Khan. He's using a false name because he's really a circus performer. He needed money, so he came to work for us. But carnivals are lower than circuses, and he doesn't want anyone to know he's working for us. We don't even know his real name, but he's a good strong man."

"I suppose that's all possible," Jupiter acknowledged. "But one thing is clear, Andy—someone is causing trouble at your carnival. We'd like to help find out who, if your Dad will let us."

Andy looked at them all. "If no one told you about all that, tell me how you found out? I don't believe in magic, no sir. How'd you do it, fellows?"

"Elementary, my dear Andy," Jupiter said, and grinned.

Bob and Pete grinned, too, as Jupiter explained what they had done to find out about the problems of the carnival. Andy was all admiration when Jupiter finished.

"Jiminy, you fellows *are* good detectives! I'll bet you *could* find out what's happening at the carnival. But carnival people are very proud, and my Dad doesn't want outside help."

"He could lose the carnival soon, Andy," Jupiter said.

"I know. If we can't pay next week—" Andy stopped and his face became determined. "All right, if Dad won't let you help, I will! Fellows, I know someone is trying to make Dad lose the carnival because of me!"

7

A Startling Discovery

"IT'S MY GRANDMOTHER! She hates Dad," Andy said.

The carnival boy's face became sad. "My mother died when I was little. She had an accident. I never really knew her too well."

"We're sorry, Andy," Bob said sympathetically.

"It happened a long time ago," Andy said. "Anyway, my grandmother—Mom's mother—never liked Dad or the carnival. She didn't want Mom to marry Dad, and when Mom died, my grandmother blamed it on Dad and the carnival. She hates the carnival, says it's no place for a boy. Well, after Mom died, Dad was kind of broken up, and the carnival wasn't doing well. I was awful young, you know? Grandma wanted me to live with her. She's not rich, but she's got some money, and Dad was moving around a lot, so he let me live with Grandma."

Andy's face darkened. "When I got older, I hated living at my grandmother's. She was nice to me, but she's scared of everything and wouldn't let me do anything! I wanted to be with Dad in the carnival. So this year I ran off and joined Dad. Jiminy, but Grandma was mad. She came after me, but she never did have me legally, so when I said I wanted to stay with the carnival, Dad told her to go home!"

Jupiter broke in, "Did she threaten trouble, Andy?"

Andy nodded. "She told Dad she'd never let me be like him and get hurt like my mother. She threatened to go to court to prove Dad couldn't take care of me. So Dad decided to try the show out here in California. That was partly to get far away from Grandma, and partly to try to make enough money to prove he could take care of me. But now, with these accidents, Dad could lose the whole show!"

Jupiter was serious. "Do you really think your grandmother would go so far as to ruin the carnival?"

"I don't know, Jupiter," Andy said slowly. "I've tried not to think about it. She was always nice to me, even if she does hate Dad. But I can't think of anyone else."

"Still, those accidents could have hurt you, Andy," Jupiter said thoughtfully. "I don't think she'd resort to such desperate measures. Maybe there's some enemy of your Dad's you don't know about. Someone with a stronger reason to ruin him."

"I don't know, Jupe, but their scheme is going to work if we don't find out," Andy said. "The whole carnival is scared about the next accident."

"The next?" Jupiter said, surprised. "But they should be feeling safer. You've had three accidents."

Andy shook his head. "They all decided that Rajah's escape doesn't count because no one was hurt and nothing bad happened, thanks to Pete. So they're still waiting for the third one."

"That's dangerous," Bob pointed out. "When people start expecting an accident they get nervous, and accidents are sure to happen."

Jupiter agreed. "That's what superstition does, fellows. What people fear will happen does happen almost all the time."

"Anyway," Pete added, "if someone's making these accidents happen, I guess there will be more."

"I think we can be sure of that, Second," Jupiter said grimly. "One thing bothers me a little. Rajah's escape isn't quite like the other two accidents. It's not the same pattern. The other two accidents happened when the carnival wasn't open. No one was there to get hurt. Only the carnival suffered. But if Pete hadn't stopped Rajah, it could have been very dangerous to other people."

"Maybe Rajah's escape *was* a real accident?" Pete said.

"No, I'm convinced it wasn't," Jupiter insisted. The stocky First Investigator frowned. "It's most baffling, fellows. When something doesn't fit a pattern, we have to look for some other pattern that everything will fit. I think it's time for us to return to the carnival. Can you get us in, Andy, even though it's not open?"

"Sure," Andy said. "I'll say you want to see the carnival rehearsing and getting ready. They all know about Pete and Rajah, so they won't be surprised."

"What do we look for, First?" Pete asked.

"I don't know for sure," Jupiter admitted. "Some kind of connection linking the three accidents, or something that looks like a new accident being planned. Anything that looks unusual or suspicious. We'll have to be careful, so—"

They all heard it—a far-off voice calling from somewhere outside. Pete hurried to the See-All.

"It's Aunt Matilda," he reported. "She wants Bob. Something about an appointment."

"My dentist's appointment!" Bob groaned. "I forgot."

Jupiter frowned. The First Investigator hated to have his plans interfered with. He sighed.

"I suppose you'd better go, Records," he said. "We'll start alone. In case we have to leave, or follow someone, we'll take my new directional signals so you can locate us."

"The new what?" Pete exclaimed.

"Directional signal and emergency alarm," Jupiter beamed proudly. "It was what I was working on yesterday, Second. I completed it this morning while waiting for you two. I only had time to finish two units, so we'll take one and Bob can take the other. It's just what we need this time. Our walkie-talkies would be too obvious. We mustn't look as if we're watching at all."

"What does your signal do, Jupe?" Andy wanted to know.

"First, it's a directional signal," Jupiter explained. "What they call a 'homer.' It bleeps at a steady rate that gets louder and faster as you get nearer to it with another signaller, and there's a dial on it that indicates direction. It's a simple arrow-dial, showing if the signal is coming from right, left or straight ahead. Each unit is a sender and receiver, and they're small enough to carry in a pocket.

"For emergencies the unit has a small, flashing red light that is activated without even being touched! It works on voice command. When one of us is in trouble, all he has to do is say the word 'help' near the unit, and the red light will flash on the other units!"

"Jiminy," Andy said with awe. "You can do almost anything, can't you, Jupiter?"

"Well, Andy"—Jupiter preened for an instant—"I try to keep our investigating work up to date. Our signal can only be picked up by our own units, and the range is three miles."

"I'll take mine and get to the carnival as soon as I can," Bob said.

Bob went out into the salvage yard to get his bike and let Aunt Matilda know that he was on his way to the dentist. Jupiter, Pete and Andy soon followed and rode off on their bikes for the carnival. The sunny day was turning grey and the wind was rising. If they hadn't been in Southern California in early September, the boys might have expected rain.

Even without rain, the day had become gloomy and brooding as the boys rode into the carnival lot.

"Andy," Jupiter instructed as they dismounted from

42

their bikes, "you go to your work so no one will become suspicious. But keep your eyes open round the shooting gallery. Pete can watch the performers rehearsing in the field over there and I'll wander round the booths and tents. Look for anything even a little strange or suspicious. Is that clear?"

Andy and Pete both nodded, and the three boys began to stroll casually to their posts among the workmen and performers.

Bob arrived at his dentist to find him busy with an emergency patient, so he had to wait. Impatient, he read all the magazines and fumed at the delay that was keeping him from the carnival.

After he had finished all the magazines, he decided to see if the early edition of the Rocky Beach evening newspaper had any story about the carnival or Rajah's escape. He found no mention of the lion, but he did find a feature story about the carnival, saying what a fine show it was and urging people to go.

Bob, whose Dad was a newspaperman on a large Los Angeles daily, knew at once that the story was what newsmen call a "hand-out". The reporter hadn't gone to the carnival at all. He had simply written the story from an information release given to him by the carnival.

This was common practice with small newspapers that couldn't spare a reporter for such a small story. All the newspaper was really interested in was helping the carnival do good business and helping local businessmen sell to the customers attracted by the carnival. Bob realized that it was lucky that no reporter had been at the carnival last night—he might have seen Pete and Rajah or heard about the incident. If Rajah's escape had been reported, the town authorities might have revoked the licence of the carnival.

Suddenly Bob's attention was caught by a small advertisement:

Special stuffed cats needed for children's home. Must be striped red-and-black, with crooked body, one eye, red collar. Will pay $25 for any stuffed cat fitting this description. Call Rocky Beach 7-2222.

Bob jumped up. The description exactly fitted the crooked cat Pete had won—and then lost—last night! Bob tore out the advertisement and ran to the door of the dentist's inner office.

"Doctor! I have to go," he cried, and before the dentist could protest, he was running out towards his bike.

8

Who Wants a Crooked Cat?

AT THE CARNIVAL, Pete had been watching for more than an hour in the grey afternoon. Nothing unusual had happened as far as the Second Investigator could tell. To look casual, he wandered round the field where all the performers rehearsed.

The two clowns were practising a different routine from the one the boys had seen last night. The tall, sad clown had a tiny broom and a long-handled dustpan. He went round sweeping up rubbish, and every time he raised the dustpan the bottom fell open, dumping out everything he had swept up. The tall clown looked gloomily at the fallen rubbish, and the fat little clown did flips of joy and ridicule.

The fire eater worked with flaming wads on the end

of his swords. As Pete watched with wide eyes, the fire eater calmly put the flaming wads into his mouth!

Khan the strong man lifted weights and tore thick books. Pete watched him particularly, but Khan did nothing suspicious.

The Great Ivan worked inside his show cage with Rajah, teaching the magnificent lion a new trick on the striped tubs the boys had painted.

Two wire walkers practised their dazzling show of skill and balance on a wire stretched between two high poles.

Pete watched it all, trying to look like a boy just interested in the feats of the performers.

But nothing happened in the open field.

Meanwhile, Jupiter had been prowling among the booths and tents where the roughnecks and booth operators were repairing and setting up for the night's opening. He missed no booth nor show tent and retraced his steps many times. But he, too, found nothing that seemed suspicious. He had stopped to watch the whirling carousel when Andy Carson joined him. Andy had finished his work at the shooting gallery.

"Don't you test the Ferris wheel, Andy?" Jupiter asked. He pointed to the motionless wheel, its gondolas covered with canvas.

"It cost too much to run," Andy explained. "We start it up just before the carnival opens and give it a trial run then."

"You have a mechanic to maintain it?"

"Sure, my Dad does that himself, Jupiter."

Jupiter was thoughtful. "It's your most important single ride. Almost the symbol of the whole show. If—"

"Jupiter!" Andy broke in, "here comes Bob! He looks excited!"

They watched as Bob pedalled up to Pete, and both boys came up to Jupiter and Andy. Bob began to talk before he was even off his bike.

"Jupe! Someone wants crooked cats!"

"Cats just like the one I lost!" Pete exclaimed.

"I don't think Pete lost it at all," Bob cried, digging into his pocket for the advertisement he had torn out of the newspaper. "I think it was stolen! Look at this, First!"

They all crowded round Jupiter as he read the small ad. The First Investigator's eyes became bright.

"It certainly sounds like Pete's crooked cat," he agreed. "Andy, how many of those crooked cats did you have?"

"Five here in Rocky Beach, Jupe," Andy said. "Pete's was the last one I gave out."

Jupiter nodded. "The last one, and Pete lost it. Or, as Bob says, maybe it was stolen. If it was, that was the second time the same cat was stolen—remember that moustached old man who stole it but dropped it. Fellows, I think we're beginning to see the pattern!"

"What pattern, First?" Bob wanted to know.

"Someone wants those crooked cats, Records," Jupiter stated firmly. "Maybe *all* of them, or just one. It explains why Rajah was let loose!"

"It does, Jupe?" Pete said. "How?"

"Why was Rajah let loose, First?" Bob asked.

"To distract us, Records!" Jupiter declared. "When that old man failed to steal the crooked cat, he must have circled back and watched the shooting gallery. He saw Pete win the cat. While the rest of us were shooting, he went and got Rajah. When you two and Andy went back to the trailer, he released Rajah near you to distract Pete. Pete dropped the cat and forgot about it while we were all busy with Rajah. As soon as we were out of the way, the old man picked it up and left with it!"

"Wow, First," Pete said, "he must have wanted that cat badly. It must be valuable and important."

"Yes, it must be," Jupiter agreed. "Andy, was there anything special about those crooked cats? Do you know why anyone would want one of them, or all of them?"

46

Andy shook his head. "I don't know why, Jupe. There's nothing special about them that I know of."

Jupiter pondered a moment while the others watched him. The stocky First Investigator chewed his lip.

"There are only three possibilities, fellows," he pronounced at last. "First, that someone wants all those cats for himself, the way the ad seems to say. Some special reason for needing cats like that. Second, that the crooked cats, taken all together, *mean* something."

"You mean like all the parrots in our 'Stuttering Parrot' case, First?" Bob said quickly.

Bob was referring to a case the boys had handled in which a group of parrots had each been taught part of a message that helped solve a mystery.

"Precisely," Jupiter declared. "And third, there could be something *on* one of the cats, or *inside* it, that is valuable, and that Andy didn't know about." He turned suddenly to the carnival boy. "Andy, did the carnival go to Mexico? Or anywhere near the border?"

"No, Jupe," Andy shook his head. "Only California."

"Why Mexico, First?" Bob asked.

"I was thinking of smugglers, Records," Jupiter explained. "Smugglers often hide things inside articles like those crooked cats. Where did you get those cats, Andy?"

"From Chicago," Andy said. "Dad bought them straight from the prize supplier there."

Jupiter frowned. "Well, there is something important about those cats, and we have to find out what. One thing puzzles me, though. Why did that old man try to steal only the *last* crooked cat? Andy, this is only your third day in Rocky Beach?"

"That's right. We've played only two shows. We came here overnight from San Mateo after our last show there."

"And just when did you give out the cats?" asked Jupe.

"Four the first night here," said Andy, "and the fifth to Pete last night."

"Why did you give out four cats the first night? Isn't that a lot of first prizes?"

"We always try to have a lot of winners the first night," Andy explained. "We want people to go home and talk about winning. It's good advertising. Actually, I let some borderline winners take crooked cats."

"The cats were always first prize?" Jupiter asked.

"Oh, no. I'm always changing the first prizes. I lost some of my best prizes in the San Mateo fire, so I made the crooked cats a first prize the first night here."

Jupiter pondered. "You keep your prizes in that trailer? How safe are they?"

"Well, the trailer is always locked. When the show isn't open, it's attached to our trucks, and it has a burglar alarm on it—we get a lot of attempts to pilfer our stuff—kids mostly. Someone's nearly always round our truck, and when the gallery is open, I keep the trailer locked behind the booth where I can see it."

"Then it would be very difficult to steal one of the cats from the trailer without being seen?"

"It sure would," Andy declared. "I mean, someone could break it open easy enough, but at night and most of the day the alarm would go off, and when the alarm's off, a thief would be almost sure to be seen. I guess a thief could break it open and run, but we'd know about it."

"Yes," Jupiter said slowly, and the boys could almost see the wheels turning in the First Investigator's brain. "So you left San Mateo with five crooked cats. You came straight here. It would have been difficult to steal the cats between San Mateo and here. It would have been difficult to steal the cats from your trailer at any time without the theft being quickly discovered. You opened up here right away, and you quickly gave away four cats as first prize. Then, last night, that old man with the moustache and dark glasses tried to grab the last cat. He failed, and Pete got it. Rajah got loose, and Pete lost that last cat. Now someone is advertising for cats just like your crooked ones."

"That's how it all happened, all right," Andy agreed. "But what does it all mean, Jupiter?"

The First Investigator's eyes took on the gleam so familiar to Bob and Pete—the gleam that told them that Jupiter was about to hatch a theory.

"One fact stands out, Andy," the stocky leader of the Investigators announced. "No attempt was made to steal any of your cats before last night, and no attempt was made to steal them from the trailer at all. To me, that suggests two strong probabilities."

Jupiter's eyes gleamed round at them all. "I'm convinced that the crooked cats became valuable only within the last few days. And I'm convinced that the man who wants those cats is a member of the carnival!"

9

Jupiter Has a Plan

"BUT JUPITER," Andy protested. "no one in the carnival looks like that old man with the moustache."

"A simple disguise, Andy," Jupiter declared. "The moustache was thick, he wore a hat to hide his face, and wore dark glasses when it was almost night."

"Gosh, First," Pete pointed out, "a carnival member could have just grabbed the cats from the trailer any time."

"Sure," Bob agreed. "He wouldn't need disguises and tricks, First. He'd just sneak up and steal the cats."

"No, Records. The very fact that no attempt was made to break into the trailer is what convinces me," Jupiter pronounced. "An outsider would have just broken in and run. Even if he had known how hard it was to steal the cats, he wouldn't have cared as long as he escaped. And he wouldn't have to worry about being recognized."

"Well?" Bob said.

"A member of the carnival would have to disguise himself or risk being seen," Jupiter went on, "and he would know how hard it was to break into that trailer. He couldn't just grab and run—he'd have been missed! And if he didn't run away, he'd risk being seen on the lot with the cats. On top of that, fellows, stealing cats from the trailer would reveal at once that they had some value to someone!"

"Gosh, Jupe," Pete exclaimed. "You mean that the thief didn't want anyone to know there'd been a theft!"

"Exactly, Second," Jupiter said triumphantly. "I think he didn't want any attention drawn to those crooked cats, because their value is somehow connected to the carnival! I'm sure the thief is afraid someone might guess their value if they were openly stolen, and that he would be in trouble. I don't see how any of that would have hurt an outsider."

"Jiminy, maybe you're right," Andy said, but he still looked doubtful.

"I know I am," Jupiter stated flatly. "The fact that the thief waited until last night to try to steal even one cat also convinces me. Because he is a member of the carnival, he had to be careful, and because he's a member, he could *afford* to wait! He wanted to pick exactly the right moment to get the cats in a way that wouldn't arouse suspicion. Only a member of the carnival could observe Andy and the trailer closely enough to feel secure in waiting for a perfect chance. Only he waited too long."

"Too long, Jupe?" Pete asked, perplexed.

"Yes. Second. You remember that Andy said the crooked cats weren't first prize until here in Rocky Beach? Then he gave out four cats that first night. He caught the thief by surprise. Four of the cats were gone. The thief had to move fast. He grabbed the last cat, but lost it. That made him desperate, and he resorted to risky tricks like releasing Rajah."

"Rajah had to be taken to where Pete would see him," Andy said eagerly. "Only someone who knew Rajah would attempt that!"

"And someone who knew Rajah was pretty safe, as Jupe said last night," Bob declared.

"He was desperate, fellows," Jupiter repeated, "and now he's even more desperate. He had to place that ad in the paper to try to find the rest of the cats, either because Pete's cat wasn't the one he wanted or because he wants them all."

Bob nodded now. "I guess you're right, First. But why did you say the crooked cats became valuable only in the last few days?"

"Because nothing happened for three weeks before that fire in San Mateo, Records," Jupiter explained. "Unless that was a real accident, everything has happened quickly after that. I think that fire could have been a first attempt to get the cats. Were the crooked cats in the booth at San Mateo, Andy?"

"Some of them, I think," Andy said. "I had them for display. I wasn't giving them out there."

"But, Jupe," said Bob. "You said the thief had been waiting for his chance. If he tried to get the cats in San Mateo, doesn't that ruin your theory?"

"Of course not," Jupiter said, a little miffed. "I said he was waiting for a good chance. Maybe he tried in San Mateo, failed, and lay low waiting for another chance.

Still, there could be some other reason for the fire. That's one of the things we have to learn, fellows. We have to learn what is going on, and who wants those crooked cats so much."

"How do we do that, First?" Pete asked eagerly.

Jupiter thought. "You will stay here, Second. Find a place from which you can see everyone who leaves the carnival without being seen yourself."

"Gee, do I have to stay here, Jupe?" Pete complained.

"Since I'm sure the thief is a member of the carnival," Jupiter instructed, "he'll have to leave to meet the people who answer his ad—unless he has a confederate. From the way he's been acting I think he's alone, and you may be able to spot something suspicious. Records, give Second your directional signal. I'll keep mine for us."

"You're going somewhere?" Andy asked. "Can I come with you?"

"All right, Andy, but we have to hurry," Jupiter said.

Pete cried, "Where're you all going, Jupe?"

His question bounced off the retreating backs of his friends as they ran to get their bicycles. When Jupiter had a plan of action, he rarely stopped to explain it to his fellow investigators. Pete glumly watched them disappear out of the carnival grounds. Alone in the grey late afternoon, he looked round for a place where he could hide and still see the main and side exits from the carnival. His gaze fell on the high fence of the abandoned amusement park some twenty yards outside the main gate of the carnival.

There were holes in the high fence here, and the beams of the old roller coaster jutted up above the fence. It looked like the perfect spot to watch the carnival without being seen. Pete glanced round, but no one seemed to be watching him. They were all too busy. The Second Investigator strolled casually from the carnival and across to a hole in the high old fence of the amusement park.

Checking once more to be sure he was unobserved, he slipped through the hole in the fence. Once inside, he made his way past the rickety abandoned buildings of other attractions of the once lively amusement park to the roller coaster. He climbed up inside the lattice of old beams that held up the roller-coaster tracks until he found a place from which he could see both carnival exits without being observed himself.

He sat braced among the beams, and settled down to watch the carnival some fifty yards away. He was uneasily aware of the silent gloom round him. Cold wind made the old wooden structures creak and groan in the emptiness, and the fence seemed to cut him off from the live world outside.

The ghostly roller coaster towered menacingly above him in the grey day. The fun house between where he sat and the fence was eerie, its entrance a giant painted mouth, wide and laughing. To the right, at the edge of the ocean, the tunnel of love sagged with holes in its walls. A narrow channel of sluggish water lapped at its entrance, where small boats had once waited to take lovers for rides.

Pete felt very alone in his perch. Then he became alert as a figure strode out of the main entrance of the carnival. It was a man who looked round and hurried away towards the business section of Rocky Beach. Pete stared after the retreating figure in dismay. There had been something familiar about him, but he had been wearing city clothes, and at fifty yards in the gloomy grey light Pete could not be sure!

Had it been Khan? Pete thought he had recognized the massive shoulders of the strong man, and maybe the beard. But if the man had wild hair it had been hidden under a hat, and without the black-and-gold tights Pete wasn't sure.

Soon after, while Pete was still alert and straining to see, another man emerged from the main exit. A tall figure, once again vaguely familiar, and once again Pete wasn't sure. Had it been The Great Ivan in his street clothes?

Pete's heart sank as he realized the truth: at fifty yards he couldn't really recognize the carnival performers out of their costumes! He didn't know them well enough.

He became certain when two more men came out of the side exit. One was old, grey-haired and tall. The other was bald and middle-aged. The second man might have been the fire eater, but the first he couldn't recognize at all.

Groaning inwardly, the Second Investigator continued to watch. As more people came out of the carnival, he realized that rehearsal times must be over. Even if he could recognize the figures, it wouldn't mean anything. Everyone in the carnival seemed to be taking a late-afternoon break.

Finally one really familiar face and figure slipped out of the side exit—Mr Carson himself. Andy's father hurried away towards a small car and drove off. Pete shifted on his perch and wondered if he should stay where he was or give up and try to find his friends.

While he tried to decide, the old amusement park's wood creaked and groaned in the rising wind.

10

The Tattooed Man

WHEN Jupiter, Bob, and Andy rode away from the carnival, leaving Pete alone to watch, the First Investigator led them straight to the salvage yard. While Bob and

Andy waited alongside their bicycles, Jupiter vanished into the mounds of junk without a word to his companions.

"What's he doing now, Bob?" Andy asked.

"I don't know," Bob admitted. "When Jupiter has some big scheme, he usually forgets to tell us what it is until we're doing it. But he knows what he's doing—I hope."

They heard banging and thudding inside the mounds of junk. Jupiter seemed to be hurling heavy objects everywhere. At last they heard a cry of triumph, and the stocky First Investigator soon emerged into the open. He wore a broad grin and carried some strange, ragged object.

"I knew we had one here," he exulted. "The Jones Salvage Yard has everything!"

He held up the most dilapidated stuffed cat Bob and Andy had ever seen. It was spotted black and white; its legs were torn, one eye was missing, and the stuffing was coming out.

"What's it for Jupiter?" Andy asked.

"Why, to answer the ad, of course," Jupiter said.

"But, Jupe," Bob objected, "that's not anything like Andy's crooked cats!"

"It will be, Records," Jupiter stated. "Come on."

He hurried into Tunnel Two and up into Headquarters, with Bob and Andy following him. He went straight to a small workbench in a corner.

"Records, call that telephone number in the ad and find out where we have to go."

While Bob made the call, Jupiter began to work on the ragged stuffed cat. He used quick drying, brush-on dye, needle and thread, and twisted pieces of wire to reconstruct and repair the cat. He worked quickly and in silence, his eyes bright with purpose. Bob hung up and joined Andy at the workbench.

55

"You have an address, Records?" Jupiter asked without looking up from his work.

"The number was an answering service," Bob said. "They told me to go to 47 San Roque Way. That's only about ten blocks from here, Jupe."

"Good. We should be in plenty of time since the ad only came out in the evening paper. He probably used the answering service because he didn't have an address when he placed that ad."

Half an hour later, Jupiter sat back in satisfaction and buckled a red-dyed collar round the stuffed cat's neck.

"There! One red-and-black, one-eyed, red-collared crooked cat. The wire twists the legs just right, I believe."

"It still doesn't look like Andy's cats," Bob decided.

"But good enough for our purposes," Jupiter declared. "Now let's go and sell a crooked cat!"

Fifteen minutes later Bob, Andy and Jupiter crouched in a grove of palm trees not far from 47 San Roque Way. It was a small stucco house set far back from the street, with a faded sign on it that showed it had once been the combination home-office of a watchmaker. It seemed deserted in the gloomy late afternoon, with no curtains at the windows and no lights inside.

The street was not deserted. A horde of boys and girls milled around with stuffed cats in their arms. The cats were of every possible description. The prospective sellers were eager, but it was clear that the door of the house was locked.

"Most of those cats are all wrong," Bob pointed out. "Can't those kids read right?"

"They all hope the buyer will make an exception for them," Jupiter said. "They all want twenty-five dollars for cats worth maybe ten dollars."

"Everyone wants something for nothing," Andy said. "All carnival people know that."

At that moment a small blue car stopped in the alley

behind the stucco house. Someone got out and hurried round to the front of the house. He was too far away and moved too quickly for the boys to get a real look at him.

The man unlocked the front door of the small house, and the horde of eager cat-sellers began to pour inside after him. Andy shifted with excitement where the boys crouched hidden among the palms.

"What do we do, Jupiter?" he asked quickly.

"First, Andy, do you recognize that blue car?"

Andy peered hard towards the distant car. "No, Jupe, I don't think I ever saw it before. Most carnival people have bigger cars than that to pull their trailers."

"Very well," Jupiter nodded. "You and I will stay here and watch. One of us can sneak round in a few minutes and examine that car. We must be careful, though, not to be seen. I don't think the thief can be aware that any-one is after him yet. Anyway, if I'm right about him being a carnival member, he would recognize you, Andy."

"What do I do?" Bob asked. "As if I didn't know."

"Yes, Records," Jupiter instructed, "you will go in and try to sell our stuffed cat. He'll refuse to buy, if my deductions are correct, but you'll see who he is and per-haps find out just what is so valuable about the crooked cats."

"Okay, First," Bob said, and remounted his bike.

Carrying the fake crooked cat, Bob pedalled up to the long front path of the stucco house. He rode on to the door and dismounted. Then he joined the stream of boys and girls still pouring into the house.

Inside, he found himself in a bare living room mobbed with the eager sellers. The only furniture was some straight chairs and a single long table. At a chair behind the table, almost hidden by the crowd of boys and girls, the man was taking the cats one by one and examining them.

"No, I'm sorry, boys, those three won't do at all," the

man said in a hoarse voice to two older boys. "You see, I must have only a certain kind of cat. No, that one won't do, either. I'm sorry. My ad made it very clear that I want specific stuffed cats."

Then the man's arm reached out quickly to take a crooked cat that looked exactly like the cat that Pete had won and then lost at the carnival. Bob stared. On the man's left forearm was a large tattoo of a sailing ship, clear and unmistakable!

"Good, that's just what I need, son," the tattooed man said as he gave the owner twenty-five dollars.

But Bob wasn't listening. He was thinking that if the man was a member of the carnival, Andy should know the tattoo! He didn't see how Andy could have missed such a mark, and if—he was looking straight into the swarthy face of the tattooed man. The man's eyes flickered, and he pointed at Bob.

"You in the red sweater. Can I see your cat?"

Bob walked up to the table, trying not to show how scared he was, but the man only reached out and took the cat. He glanced at the fake cat, then smiled up at Bob.

"Well, it's been repaired, but it's a good job. My kids at the home will like it. Here's your money, son."

Stunned, Bob took the twenty-five dollars without really knowing what was happening. He found himself staring at the tattooed man, but, fortunately, the man immediately returned to looking at other cats. Recovering himself, Bob backed away from the table.

As he did, he saw the pile of stuffed cats on the floor behind the table. One was his own, and one wasn't any more like the cat Pete had lost than his was. But the other two were identical to Pete's prize.

The stream of kids was thinning now, and Bob hesitated. He was torn between leaving before he attracted attention and staying to see if he could learn more about the crooked cats. He decided to risk staying a little longer.

"I need cats to match a giant cat the children's home has as a kind of mascot," the tattooed man explained to some disappointed boys. "It was made in Germany a long time ago. We want similar cats to give to all our kids as Christmas presents."

"Gee," a boy who had just failed said, "maybe I know who has one like you want, mister. My friend Billy Mota won a cat at the carnival."

"Did he?" the tattooed man said. "Unfortunately, I suppose he didn't see my ad, and I only have today."

"He lives near me, 39 Chelham Place," the boy blurted out.

"I won't have time, son," the tattooed man said.

For an instant, Bob was certain that the swarthy man's dark eyes had flickered towards him. But he could not be sure that it hadn't been his imagination. The crowd in the room had dwindled to a very few boys, and Bob realized that soon he would be too obviously hanging round after selling his cat.

Quietly, as the tattooed man was eagerly buying one more cat that looked exactly like the one Pete had lost, Bob slipped through the door. On his bike he rode back to the grove of palms. Jupiter and Andy greeted him anxiously.

"You were in there a long time," Andy said.

'I was trying to see if I could learn what was valuable about those cats, but I couldn't," Bob explained. "But I did see the man. Andy, he's pretty tall and swarthy, and he's got a tattoo of a sailing ship on his left arm! Have you ever seen a man like that at the carnival?"

"A tattooed sailing ship?" Andy frowned. "No, Bob, never. Some of the roughnecks are tattooed, but not like that. I don't know anyone who sounds like that man."

Jupiter was thoughtful. "He probably keeps the tattoo

hidden at the carnival, and the way he looked to you, Bob, is maybe another disguise. Andy searched his car, but found no clues at all. We took the licence number, though."

"I have something more important, Jupe," Bob said. "He bought our cat!"

Jupiter was incredulous. "He bought it? The fake?"

Bob displayed the twenty-five dollars. "He bought five cats, all told. Three of them looked like Andy's cats, but ours and one other didn't. What's he doing, Jupe?"

"Did he recognize you, do you think?" Jupiter asked.

"How could he? I never saw him before."

"Unless he was that old thief last night," Jupiter pointed out. "If he did recognize you, he might have bought wrong cats to fool us."

"You said he only got three like mine?" Andy asked.

"That's all, but some boy told him about another kid who won a cat at your carnival. He got the address of the other kid, and so did I: Billy Mota, 39 Chelham Place."

"Good work, Records," Jupiter said. "If he is after the carnival cats, and the three he bought don't turn out to be what he wants, he'll have to go after that fourth cat. We'll go to Billy Mota, too, but first we have to see what he does with the cats he has, and if he finds——"

Andy broke in, "I think the last boy is leaving!"

They watched as a solitary boy came out of the house still carrying a blue-and-white stuffed cat. The tattooed man appeared at the front door, looked up and down the quiet street, then went back inside. The sound of the door lock snapping shut carried to the boys.

"Come on," Jupiter whispered.

The grey day was growing dark early as they slipped up to the stucco house. At the living-room window they carefully raised their heads to look inside.

"There he is," Bob whispered.

The swarthy tattooed man sat at the long table. On

60

the table in front of him were three crooked cats, all exactly like the one Pete had lost. The tattooed man was examining each of them in turn.

"They're my crooked cats, all right," Andy whispered.

"Look in the corner!" Jupiter said.

On the floor behind the table were two more cats—the stuffed cats that were not like Pete and Andy's.

Jupiter said, "He's thrown those aside! He does want only your carnival cats, Andy."

"Shhhhhh!" Bob warned low.

Jupiter's voice had risen as he realized that the tattooed man was really after the carnival cats. In the room, the man flung down the last cat, and stood up with a long, wicked knife gleaming in his hand.

11

Trapped !

UNABLE TO MOVE, the boys peered in the window as the tattooed man stood over the table with his long knife.

Suddenly, he began to slash at the first crooked cat with the knife. He cut into the second cat, and the third. He stared at the crooked cats, and then began to fling the stuffing all over the table. With his hands moving frantically, he pawed over the stuffing and the pieces of covering.

Breathing hard, the tattooed man dropped his knife and slumped down in the chair behind the table. He looked with gloomy hatred at the hacked remains of the three crooked cats.

Bob whispered, "He didn't find what he wants!"

"No," Jupiter agreed, "but whatever he's looking for is something inside the cats—or *one* of the cats. And that means it has to be inside the last missing cat! The one that Billy Mota has! If we hurry, we can get there before—"

"Jupiter!" Andy cried. "He's coming out!"

Inside the room the tattooed man had jumped up again. His angry eyes glanced all round the room. Then he reached for a hat on a chair.

"Quick, fellows, those bushes!" Jupiter muttered.

They dived for the cover of three thick hibiscus bushes and lay flat in their shadow. The front door closed, and the tattooed man came hurrying round the house. He didn't even glance towards them, but strode past to the back alley. He vanished from their sight, and moments later they heard a car door open and close. The car engine started and roared away out of the alley.

"He's gone to get that last crooked cat, First!" Bob guessed.

"Maybe we can catch up with him," Andy said.

"On bicycles?" Bob pointed out. "Chelham Place is over five miles from here, Andy, near your carnival."

The boys all looked at each other in despair.

"He'll get the last crooked cat," Bob moaned. "And we can't stop him."

"I guess we can't," Jupiter agreed. He got up from under the hibiscus bushes and looked glumly at the small house. Then his eyes lighted up. "Or maybe we can! Fellows, look at those wires! The house has a telephone!"

Without waiting for an answer, the First Investigator ran to the front door. It was locked.

"The windows!" Andy cried.

The carnival boy tried a living-room window. It was open! He pushed it up and the three boys tumbled inside.

"Find the telephone," Jupiter urged. "Look everywhere!"

"There, Jupiter," Andy pointed. "On the floor in that corner."

Jupiter grabbed the receiver, lifted it to his ear, and listened. His face fell.

"It's not working."

"Now what do we do?" Bob asked.

"I don't know, Records," Jupiter said glumly. "Perhaps if we rode over there as fast as we could we'd still be in time, if—" he added lamely, "if no one was home when the tattooed man got there."

"He'd just break in, Jupe," Bob said.

Andy said, "There must be a public telephone somewhere near here, Jupiter!"

Jupiter groaned. "Of course, I should have—"

The stocky First Investigator never finished what he was going to say. Outside the house, coming slowly closer, the boys all heard soft, careful footsteps. They froze in fright as they listened to the ominous steps. Bob crouched low and crept silently to a front window. He looked out, ducked and hurried back.

"The tattooed man! He's coming back!"

"The window," Andy whispered urgently.

"No time, fellows," Bob said, scared.

"Quick, then, the other room!" Jupiter decided hurriedly.

They fell over each other in their haste to get to the rear room. Andy reached it first, with Bob and Jupiter sprawling in behind him. It was a small, completely bare room, with shutters over the window that made it pitch dark. They quickly closed the door and stood behind it, holding their breath.

Outside in the living-room the outer door opened and closed.

There was a long silence.

Suddenly, a rasping voice laughed just outside the back-room door. A low, nasty laugh.

"So, some smart lads, eh? Well, we'll have to see that you don't get too smart for your own good, boys."

The three boys looked at each other in dismay. There was another laugh from outside the door.

"Thought I didn't see you at the window, did you? Well, you'll have to be a lot smarter than you are to fool me. I saw you, all right. A fine trio of fools you are. Didn't even hear me park up the street. Well, you'll have time to think about your foolishness, eh?"

There was the sound of a key turning in the lock in the door of the back room, and a heavy sliding noise as something solid dropped across the door—a metal bar.

"There, that should hold you," the hoarse voice said. "But take a warning, smart boys. When you get out, stay away from me!"

There was no laugh this time. The boys heard footsteps going away and the slamming of the front door. A heavy silence descended over the small house.

"The window," Jupiter said, undaunted.

He felt his way in the dark to the window, pushed it up, reached to open the outside shutters—and stopped.

"The window's barred," he cried. "This must have been a storeroom for the watchmaker who lived here!"

"Open the shutters and yell," Bob said.

They all yelled out into the grey, darkening sky. No one came. The small house was far from the street, and the houses across the back alley were some distance away on the next street. After some minutes, Andy sat down on the floor—and noticed something in the grey light from the window that they'd missed before.

"Look! There's a back door!"

Jupe rushed over to it. The back door was double-locked and solid.

"We're stuck, fellows, and that tattooed man is sure to

get the last crooked cat now!" Andy moaned. "We're finished."

"Perhaps not!" Jupiter said suddenly. "You forgot my new signal. Pete will see the red light, and the directional signal will lead him to us."

The stocky First Investigator took out the tiny instrument he had built and bent close over it.

"Help," he said into it. "Help."

The small instrument began to hum very low.

"It lights only on the receiving instrument," Jupiter explained.

They all watched the humming signal and wondered if Pete would see the call for help.

Where Pete sat up in the beams of the old roller coaster, the sharp wind from the mountains made him shiver. He could barely see the exits from the carnival in the early dusk of the gloomy day.

None of the people he had seen leave had come back, and the carnival would open in not much more than an hour. Where were the carnival people he had watched leave, and where were Jupiter, Bob and Andy? Andy was supposed to be in his booth before the carnival opened, and it wasn't like Jupiter or Bob to stay away so long without at least trying to send a message.

Pete was worried.

Sometimes, Jupiter's tendency to keep his plans secret so that he could astound them all annoyed Pete. It was, he knew, only the First Investigator's love of the dramatic, but it had got the boys into tight corners before. He hated to leave his post, but he was uneasy now.

He climbed down from the roller coaster and hurried through the dilapidated amusement park. The enormous, laughing mouth of the Fun House seemed to leer at him as he passed it and went on to slip back through the hole in the fence.

C

At the carnival the Ferris wheel gondolas were being uncovered. The carousel was already playing its gay music. Andy Carson was not at his booth. Pete chewed on his lower lip. Where were they? He suspected that Jupiter had taken them to the man who wanted to buy crooked cats, but where was that? Some sixth sense told Pete that something was wrong.

If they came back to the carnival, they would expect to find him at his post. They would, perhaps, want his report at once. If he left his post and went looking for them, he could miss them, and they could return to the carnival to find him gone. On the other hand, if they needed help, he—

Pete remembered the new directional-and-emergency signal!

He dug into his pocket and brought out the tiny instrument. He stared at it eagerly. But it was silent. The red emergency light was dark.

12

A Human Fly

IN the locked storeroom of the small house, Andy looked up at Jupiter from the floor.

"How far does that signal reach, Jupe?"

"Three miles," Jupiter said, and suddenly groaned again. "Of course, the carnival is almost five miles from here! Pete won't get our signal!"

They all looked at each other.

"Someone'll hear us yelling, fellows," Bob said, trying to make his voice optimistic.

"Of course they will," Jupiter said firmly. "But in the meantime, we can try to find a way out ourselves. The experts say there's no such thing as a room you can't get out of somehow. There's always a flaw in a room. Come on, let's find it."

"But how, Jupe?" Andy asked. "We've looked."

"There's always a chance that we've missed something," Jupiter declared. "Bob, you examine all the walls for weak spots, places where pipes go through, anything. I'll check the window more closely, and Andy can recheck the doors and that cupboard in the corner."

Despite their pessimism, Andy and Bob couldn't help being convinced by Jupiter's staunch refusal to give up. They set to work with renewed vigour. But Andy soon decided once again that there was no way out through the solid doors, and Bob found no weak places in any of the walls.

"Keep trying, fellows!" Jupiter urged. "There must be some weakness in this room."

The First Investigator continued to study the barred window, and from time to time yelled out for help. Bob got down on his hands and knees to examine the walls at the floor. Andy went into the single cupboard.

"Jupe! Bob! Look here!"

The carnival boy held a typewritten sheet of paper he had found in the cupboard.

"It's a complete itinerary of the carnival," Andy told them. "Our whole route and schedule in California."

"Then the tattooed man *is* part of the carnival!" Jupiter said in triumph.

"Or at least he's following the carnival pretty closely," Bob said.

"Andy," Jupiter exclaimed, "did you recognize his voice? You didn't recognize the tattoo, or his face, but think about his voice!"

"No," Andy said slowly, "I'm sure I've never heard that voice before, Jupiter."

Jupiter thought a minute. "He could be disguising his voice, too. It had that odd rasp."

After looking at the carnival itinerary, Bob began to rummage round in the long, narrow cupboard that was partly filled with old boards and boxes. Suddenly he came out with some strange clothes in his hands.

"Look at this, fellows. I found it all just dropped on the floor."

Bob held up a pair of strange, black overalls that were cut very narrow, like tights; a black hoodlike head covering that fitted a whole head but left the face open; and a pair of black canvas shoes with odd rubber soles that looked a little like curved suction cups.

Jupiter frowned. "It looks like some kind of costume, Records. Perhaps a carnival costume, but I don't recall any costume like that. Andy?"

Andy was staring at the black garments with a puzzled expression. He took them and studied them.

"Well, what is it, Andy?" Jupiter wanted to know.

Andy shook his head. "None of our people wears a costume like this, but—" The carnival boy hesitated, shook his head. "I can't be sure, fellows, but I think this looks a lot like a costume the Amazing Gabbo used to wear."

"The Amazing who?" Bob said, staring.

"Gabbo," Andy said. "When I was just a little kid, right after my Mom died but before I went to Grandma, my Dad worked a little while with a small circus near Chicago. The Amazing Gabbo worked in the show, too, for a few days. We never knew him, really, and he wasn't around long. I only remember him because he was caught stealing from the circus and fired. I think he got into worse trouble later and went to prison."

"Prison?" Jupiter said quickly. "Then he could be a thief! Did he look like that tattooed man, Andy?"

"I don't know, Jupe. I guess his age is about right. But I wouldn't remember what he looked like. I don't think Dad would, either. I mean not right away unless someone told him to look for Gabbo. I guess we really never saw him out of his costume."

"And this looks like his costume?" Jupiter asked.

Andy nodded. "It sure does, I think. And those shoes are a special kind used by human flies in their acts. You know, so they can climb almost any wall."

Jupiter gaped. "A human fly?"

"Sure," Andy said. "That was Gabbo's act. He—"

But Jupiter was no longer listening. "That old man who tried a grab your crooked cat last night! He got out of that dead-end area. The only way out was to climb that high fence. No one could climb a fence like that—except, maybe, a trained human fly!"

"And Gabbo would know how to handle a lion!" Andy said.

"But, fellows," Bob said, "Andy already told us he doesn't know the tattooed man."

"The tattooed man could be another disguise, Records," Jupiter pointed out. "We must get out of here! If he gets to the fifth cat and escapes, we may never find him! Yell, fellows!"

They began to yell at the window again. But their voices echoed without response.

Pete coasted into the salvage yard on his bicycle. He had made his decision some half an hour ago—he would look for the other boys.

But as he rode into the yard in the gathering dusk, all he saw was Konrad taking the last of a load off the small truck.

"Have you seen Bob or Jupiter, Konrad?" Pete cried out to the big Bavarian helper of Uncle Titus Jones.

"I don't think I see them for a long time today, Pete," Konrad replied stolidly. "There is something wrong?"

"I don't know, I—"

Konrad raised a massive hand. "Wait, Pete. What is that strange noise? I think it is close around somewhere."

The big Bavarian looked all around him, perplexed. Pete listened and heard the strange, muffled sound—a steady, low *beeeeeeeeeeeeeeeeeeeeee*! It seemed to come from somwhere close to—his pocket!

"The signal!" Pete cried, and dug into his pocket to pull out the tiny instrument.

He stared at the flashing red light on the signaller.

"Konrad, they're in trouble!" Pete exclaimed, and he explained the signal device to the big Bavarian.

"Come on, Pete!" Konrad roared. "We go find them!"

The big Bavarian jumped into the cab of the truck and pulled Pete in beside him. While Konrad drove out of the salvage yard, Pete watched the direction pointer on the small dial of Jupiter's signal device.

"Left, Konrad!" Pete instructed, and as they reached the first corner, "Left again, yes, and now straight ahead!"

Konrad drove steadily and Pete watched the dial pointer. The direction of the signal Pete was receiving was at an angle to the grid pattern of the streets. Since they couldn't travel in a straight line as the crow flies, they had to zigzag their way towards the source of the signal. Pete kept directing Konrad to turn at corners.

"Right now, Konrad! Left, and left again. Now right!"

In a series of turns like steps, the big Bavarian drove the truck closer to the source of the signal.

"The signal's real strong now, Konrad!" Pete cried.

They had turned into a quiet street that was deserted in the dusk. Konrad drove more slowly, as Pete stared at both sides of the silent street. He saw nothing. He looked at the arrow pointer on the signal dial.

"It's to the right, Konrad, and awful close!"

Konrad peered around, worried. "I see nothing, Pete."

"Wait!" Pete cried. "It's behind us. The signal sound is lower."

Konrad applied the brakes with a screech and threw the truck gears into reverse. The truck backed slowly along the quiet street. Pete pointed to a small stucco house set far back from the roadway.

"I think it's that house, Konrad!"

Konrad had stopped the truck, and was climbing out, before Pete finished talking.

"Come on, Pete! We find them!" the big Bavarian roared, and charged across the pavement towards the small house.

Pete raced after him and reached the front door just as Konrad began to pound on it.

"It is locked, Pete! I hear no sounds! If—"

The Bavarian left the rest of his sentence unfinished. Pete stared at the locked door and the dark, silent house. Konrad backed off, his face grim as he prepared to break the door in. Pete stopped him.

"Wait, Konrad. I know how to find out if they're here," Pete said quickly. He bent over his tiny signal device and spoke into it. "Help. Help."

Instantly, like an echo, cries came from the back of the small house: *"Help! Pete! At the back!"*

Pete and Konrad hurried round the house to the rear. Konrad's great hands ripped at the back door and soon broke it open from outside. Moments later Jupiter, Bob and Andy stood grinning at their friends.

"We saw our red light go on and knew you were near, Pete," Bob exclaimed.

"That's what I figured," Pete said. "That signal worked—"

Pete stopped as a short old man advanced angrily on them from the direction of the street. He was waving his arms.

71

"What are you doing to my house!" the old man cried. "I'll have you in court for destroying my property!"

Jupiter stepped up to the angry old man. "We're sorry we had to break your door, sir, but a man locked us inside. We yelled, but no one heard us. A tattooed man, very swarthy, locked us in the back room. Is he your tenant, sir?"

"Locked in? Tattooed man? What are you talking about?" the old man said. "Why I rented the house this morning, to a very respectable man. An older man. A salesman. He had no tattoo. Who would lock you in here? That's ridiculous. Why, I'll report this!"

"That would be wise, sir. The police should know about this," Jupiter agreed. "I suggest you do it at once, sir."

The old man nodded, confused, and began to walk away. Jupiter waited only for a moment. Then he started towards the waiting truck.

"Hurry, fellows, there may still be time to get that last crooked cat! Konrad, put the bikes on the truck and drive to 39 Chelham Place! Hurry!"

13

A Near Miss

KONRAD wheeled the truck into the tree-shaded street of big, old houses not more than a block from the ocean. The boys saw no trace of a blue car on the street.

"I knew we'd never catch up with him, First," Bob said, dejected.

"You were locked in too long, Jupe," Pete agreed.

"There is always the chance that something will hold him up," Jupiter insisted. "That must be number 39 up at the end of the street. And, fellows, it's dark!"

It was a three-storey white house surrounded by tall trees and flower beds. It was dark in the early dusk, as Jupiter had said. A car was parked in the driveway, but it wasn't a small blue car. As Konrad drove closer, lights went on inside the house.

"Someone must have just come home?" Jupiter declared.

Konrad slowed the truck to park in front of the house. Suddenly a woman's cries shattered the twilight:

"Thief! Stop him! Police!"

Konrad jammed on the brakes and had the truck door open before the truck had come to a full stop.

"The tattooed man must be in there!" Pete cried.

"Hurry, fellows!" Jupiter urged.

They all leaped from the truck, but Konrad was first. The big Bavarian waved them back.

"I take good care of him, boys! Stay behind me!"

They began to run towards the house where the woman was still crying out. Then Pete stopped and pointed up among the trees to the side of the house.

"Look!" he cried.

They all saw the shadowy figure in the dusk coming swiftly down the sheer side of the house. As they watched, the figure swarmed down from unseen handhold to handhold, and dropped to the ground in a pool of light from a downstairs window. It was the swarthy, tattooed man—and he carried a large black-and-red bundle.

"It's him!" Bob exclaimed. "He's got the crooked cat!"

Andy shouted, furious, "Stop, you thief!"

The man's head jerked round at Andy's shout. He saw the boys and Konrad, and whirled instantly towards the rear of the house. He disappeared among the back-garden trees. Konrad bellowed like a bull and pounded in pursuit.

"I get him, boys!" Konrad yelled.

But the tattooed man was faster than Konrad or the boys, and vanished into the next street while they were still among the trees. Pete was the first to reach the next street. He stood staring helplessly as the others panted up. They all watched as far up the street the small blue car started and quickly roared away out of sight.

"We had him, and we lost him!" Pete moaned.

"He got my last crooked cat, too!" Andy wailed.

"We got his licence number earlier," Bob pointed out eagerly. "The police can trace him!"

"That would take some time, Records," Jupiter said, crest-fallen. "But possibly in his haste he left some clue at the house! Come on, fellows, hurry!"

As they reached the big white house, a pretty woman was standing on the side steps with a small boy behind her. Her eyes were wide with alarm, and she looked suspiciously at the boys and Konrad.

"Do you boys know that awful man?" she demanded.

"We do, Ma'am," Jupiter declared. "He is a nefarious thief we have been attempting to apprehend. We traced him to your house, but we came just too late."

The woman stared. "You've been trying to catch a criminal like that? Why, you're only boys!"

Jupiter frowned in annoyance. The First Investigator had long resented the assumption of adults that because they were "only boys," they were without intelligence or ability, and therefore unimportant.

"It is true we are 'only boys', Ma'am," Jupiter said a little stiffly, "but I assure you that we have much experience solving puzzles and crimes. I presume you are Mrs Mota?"

"Why, yes," Mrs Mota said, startled. "How on earth did you know my name?"

The figure dropped to the ground in a pool of light . . .

"We knew that man was coming here," Jupiter explained. "Unfortunately, he delayed us. We really didn't expect to find him still here, but I gather that you have just come home?"

"Yes," Mrs Mota nodded. "Billy and I were out. We came home only a few minutes ago. Billy went straight up to his room, and the next thing I knew he was calling for help!"

The small boy, no more than ten years old, said eagerly, "He was up on the stairs to the top floor! He jumped down when he saw me and grabbed my crooked cat!"

"Of course, you had the crooked cat with you!" Jupiter understood in a flash. "That was why he was still here! He couldn't find the cat in the house, so he had to wait!"

"After he had Billy's cat," Mrs Mota went on, "he started down, saw me, and ran up to the second floor. That was when I began to call for help."

Pete said, "And he climbed out of the second-floor window and down the wall!"

"Like a human fly!" Bob exclaimed.

"Billy," Jupiter said, "Did you find anything on that crooked cat? Or anything inside it?"

"Nope," Billy Mota said. "I guess I never looked."

The boys all looked glumly at each other. The last crooked cat was in the hands of the tattooed man. They stood in the dusk trying to think of what they could do next.

"He got what he wanted," Bob said. "We'll never find him."

"We could still get the licence number of his car traced," Pete said hopefully.

"That will take time, Second," Jupiter said again. "It has to be sent to Sacramento. Perhaps we should—"

Konrad, who had been standing silently by all this time, now stepped up to Jupiter and broke in.

"We now call the police, Jupiter."

Jupiter protested, "But, Konrad, by the time—"

Konrad shook his head. "You call the police now. Your Uncle Titus would say that, too. This lady is robbed, her house broken in. The man is dangerous, I think. We have lost him. It is now for the police."

Bob agreed. "We can't catch him now, Jupe."

"We'd better call Chief Reynolds, First?" Pete said.

Jupiter sighed and his shoulders dropped. "I suppose you're right. May we use your telephone, Mrs Mota?"

"Of course you can, boys," Mrs Mota said.

They all trooped inside, and Jupiter called Chief Reynolds. It didn't take long. The Chief respected anything the boys reported. Jupiter started to hang up.

"He'll be right over here, and—" Jupiter stared at the receiver in his hands. "Andy! Call your father at the carnival! Find out if anyone is missing!"

"Missing?" Andy frowned. "Jiminy, Jupe, I told you I never saw that man before."

"We agreed he is probably in disguise," Jupiter said. "That swarthy face could be a mask, and a tattoo can be hidden. Find out if everyone is at the carnival!"

"Well, all right," Andy said, dubiously, "but my Dad's awful busy just before the show opens, and it's hard to be sure who's there or not."

"Try, Andy!" Bob urged.

Andy went to the telephone, and dialled. He listened for a time as the phone rang and rang.

"He's not in the office, fellows," the carnival boy said. "I'll try the box office, and see if they can find Dad."

Andy was still on the telephone when they heard police cars screech to a stop outside. Konrad looked relieved. Chief Reynolds himself strode into the house with some of his men. The boys quickly told the Chief their whole story.

"Good work, boys," Chief Reynolds said. "With your description and the licence number we should be able to catch the thief. Now, do you have any idea what he is after in those crooked cats?"

"No, sir," Bob admitted.

."But it must be awful valuable, the trouble he's taking," Pete added. "Jupe thinks maybe it's something smuggled!"

Chief Reynolds nodded. "That is a very good thought. I'll instruct my men to be alert for a valuable item inside the cat, and send out a call for any information the border patrol might have on a wanted smuggler."

The Chief hurried out to the rest of his men. Andy Carson was still trying to get through to his father at the carnival. Jupiter, who was disappointed at having to call in Chief Reynolds before the boys even knew why the cats were valuable, watched Andy nervously.

"He would have had time to get back to the carnival by now," the First Investigator said in dejection. "Unless, of course, he doesn't go back at all this time," he added hopefully. "Keep trying, Andy."

Andy nodded, and dialled once more, just as Chief Reynolds came back into the house. The Chief was walking fast, his face serious as he approached the boys.

"Boys, you may have stumbled on to something far more important than you know! I've just had a report that a man who answers your cat-thief's description, tattoo and all, is suspected of a daring one-man bank robbery only last week! He escaped with over $100,000!"

Jupiter cried quickly, "In San Mateo, sir?"

"What?" Chief Reynolds said, looking at Jupiter. "Now, how did you know that, Jupiter?"

"The fire at the carnival, sir! It was in San Mateo. I'm convinced that the cat-thief is a member of the carnival. He must have set off the fire by accident after the robbery, or maybe on purpose to help him to escape!"

"You can't be sure of that, Jupiter," the Chief said.

"The coincidence would be too much, Chief," Jupiter insisted. "If you go to the carnival, you'll—"

78

Andy cried out, "I've got my Dad!"

They all stopped to listen as the carnival boy spoke eagerly into the telephone, and they waited impatiently as Andy's Dad checked who was at the carnival. Chief Reynolds left the room again when one of his men called him. Moments later, Andy was nodding into the telephone.

"Yes, Dad. Jiminy, I'm sorry! But is anyone missing? No, all right. Yes, Dad. Right away!"

Andy hung up. "Everyone's there, Jupiter. At least they are now—all except me! The show's already open. I've got to get there right away. I won't even have time for dinner."

Bob and Pete both jumped as if shot, their faces pictures of dismay.

"Oh my gosh," Pete moaned, "we've missed our dinners!"

"We're in real trouble, Jupe," Bob echoed.

Jupiter, too, paled a little. Konrad chuckled at the thought of what Aunt Matilda would say to Jupe. The boys knew that nothing annoyed their parents and guardians more than missing dinner, no matter what tight spots their investigating work got them into. But Jupiter hated to leave before Chief Reynolds could tell them something more. So the boys stood there nervously until the Chief returned. He nodded grimly to them.

"We don't have to go to the carnival, boys," the Chief announced. "We just found the car only four blocks from here in the highway. The crooked cat was in the car. It had been cut open, there was nothing in it. Tyre marks on the grass show he was either picked up by another car, or had a second car ready and waiting. Anyway, we'll have to alert the whole state now. I'm afraid he got what he wanted and left Rocky Beach in a hurry, boys. I guess you'd better go home. We'll get him, but it will take time now."

The boys nodded dejectedly. They hurried down to the

truck with Konrad, more worried now about being late than about losing the cat-thief.

Or, rather, Bob, Pete and Andy were worried. Jupiter was thinking about something else, something interesting. His eyes were speculative, but no one noticed.

14

Jupiter Makes Deductions

FOR MISSING THEIR DINNERS, both Bob and Pete spent all next day performing chores around their houses. They had to admit that they'd asked for it, and worked without too much grumbling, but their minds were on the failure of the case. They couldn't help wondering if the tattooed man had been caught. Each tried to call Jupiter more than once, but the First Investigator wasn't at Headquarters or at his house.

At dinner, Bob gulped his food. His father smiled at him.

"Chief Reynolds reports that you and your friends almost caught a bank robber last night," Mr Andrews said.

"We didn't know he was a bank robber, Dad," Bob explained. "We were just helping a carnival boy in trouble."

"It's good to help people, Bob, and I know that you boys are careful. Chief Reynolds says you did nothing foolish or dangerous. Still, you worry me sometimes. Be sure you keep alert and use your head, son."

"Jupiter says being prepared is half the fight."

"As usual, Jupiter is right," Mr Andrews said drily.

"Too bad your man escaped. Chief Reynolds says he's been reported all over the state, but they haven't caught him."

This news did nothing to cheer Bob. As he rode to the salvage yard after dinner, he realized that this could turn out to be the first unsolved case The Three Investigators had ever had. He was still brooding over it when he clambered up into Headquarters. Jupiter was there, bent intently over a pile of newspapers and studying some scrawled notes.

"What are you doing, First?" Bob asked.

The First Investigator shook his head curtly to indicate that he didn't want to talk. Miffed, Bob began to study some specimens of sea life the boys had gathered while skin diving. Then he wandered to the See-All and began to survey the salvage yard in the fading light of the sunny day.

"Looks like Uncle Titus has bought another load no one knows what to do with," he announced.

Jupiter grunted. He had stopped his reading and was sitting deep in thought, his eyes closed. Bob looked back through the See-All.

"Here comes Pete!"

This time Jupiter didn't even grunt. Soon Pete came up through the trapdoor and stared at the silent Jupiter.

"What's Jupe doing?" he wanted to know.

"Don't ask me," Bob replied. "The Great Brain is at work."

"Why all the newspapers? Is he going to find the tattooed man by putting another ad in the paper?"

Jupiter looked up, his eyes bright. "That won't be needed, Second. I think I know where the tattooed man is."

"You do, Jupe?" Bob cried. "Where?"

"Where he's been all the time—here in Rocky Beach, at the carnival."

Pete groaned. "Gosh, Jupe, like Chief Reynolds said, we don't know that. Why, he's been seen in six different places!"

"Seven, to be precise," Jupiter agreed.

"That proves he's sure not here," Bob said.

"On the contrary, Records," Jupiter pronounced. "I've been studying the reports on him in the papers. The seven people saw him in seven different places as much as two hundred miles apart! I would venture to say that no one has seen him!"

Bob nodded. "I see that, Jupe. But what makes you so sure he's still in Rocky Beach, and at the carnival?"

Jupiter jumped up and began to pace the tiny room. "I've read everything I could find about the bank robbery. There are three items—two in the San Mateo paper and one in a Los Angeles paper. I also took a trip to San Mateo today while you two were paying for missing dinner."

"Why didn't you have to work?" Pete demanded hotly. "You missed dinner, too!"

"I did have to work," Jupiter said, and grinned. "But it just happened that I knew of some very interesting junk that could be purchased in San Mateo. When I told Uncle Titus about the junk there, he sent me to get it with Hans and Konrad."

Pete sighed. "Some people are just lucky, I guess. Nothing ever gets me out of working around the house."

"What did you learn about the robbery, First?" Bob asked.

"Well," Jupiter said, his face eager now, "it happened on the Friday night of the carnival fire, all right. On Fridays, the San Mateo bank is open until six o'clock, the weekend deposits are large, and the carnival opens earlier than usual! Also, fellows, that Friday was the carnival's last day in San Mateo! They were due to leave San Mateo late than night, travel here, and open on Saturday night!"

"Gosh," Pete said. "Just right if a member of the carnival wanted to rob the bank and get away fast!"

"Exactly, Second," Jupiter said. "The robber of the bank was dressed all in black, with a close-fitting black hood and black tennis shoes."

"Gabbo's costume!" Bob exclaimed.

Jupiter nodded. "Only the robber's *arms* were bare. All the witnesses agreed on that. The robber had rolled up his sleeves."

"That's how everyone noticed the tattoo," Bob realized.

"Yes, Records," Jupiter said. "The robber entered the bank at five minutes before six. He captured a guard and went into the open vault where the money was. He held the guard hostage until he was outside. Then he stunned the guard and ran into an alley beside the bank. The alarm had been turned on the moment he left the bank, and a police car arrived within minutes."

"But he got away, didn't he, Jupe?" Pete asked impatiently.

"He got away, but they don't know how!" Jupiter said. "The police ran into that alley within minutes after the robber. They didn't find him—and yet it was a totally blind alley! There was no way out of that alley at all. Only three building walls with high, locked windows. Yet the robber was gone!"

"Just like when we chased that moustached man!" Bob said.

"He climbed a wall," Pete exclaimed. "A human fly!"

"That is what I believe," Jupiter nodded. "The San Mateo police put out the alarm and looked for the robber. They found no trace of him until they had a fortunate piece of luck. A policeman on duty outside the carnival—a policeman who had been told about the bank robber—went to stop a scuffle among the people waiting to get into the carnival. In the mêlée a man wearing a raincoat was knocked down, and his coat flew open. The policeman saw a tight black costume under the coat, and glimpsed a tattoo under the sleeve of the coat!"

"Wow, that was real luck, Jupe?" Pete declared.

"Yes," the First Investigator agreed, "but many crimes are solved by such small mischances, Second. Anyway, the man wearing the raincoat got away in the crowd. The policeman called for help, and other police rushed over to the carnival. They cordoned off the area, and moved in. They were sure they would find the robber, but—"

"I know," Bob said quickly, "the fire broke out!"

"It did," Jupiter said in triumph. "That was a great danger, so the police had to help put it out. When they had the fire out, they continued their search, but they didn't find the robber or the money. Yet I'm certain he was there!"

"Why, Jupe?" Bob asked.

"Well, the robber had escaped. He was safe. His only problem was to get out of San Mateo unseen. To go out in the open at the carnival would have been very foolish of him—unless he was a member of the carnival who had planned all along to escape from San Mateo *with* the carnival. I'm convinced that his whole plan was to rob the bank, escape up the wall of that alley, then slip back into the carnival and remove his disguise. A simple and very safe plan."

"Only he was accidentally spotted," Bob went on, "and then he had to have time to get out of his disguise. So he started the fire to gain time and distract everyone— the same sort of idea as letting Rajah loose later."

Pete asked, "You mean the way he looked at the bank in San Mateo, and every time we've seen him, he's been in a disguise?"

"I do," Jupiter stated somewhat pompously. "At the bank, and in that house where he bought the crooked cats, his face was stained swarthy, or he had on a plastic mask. His hair was darkened, perhaps his nose changed—and he had a false tattoo!"

Bob and Pete didn't say anything for a full minute. Then Pete exclaimed:

"Gosh, a tattoo is something everyone remembers!"

Bob added, "They'd hardly remember anything else once they'd seen that tattoo. We hardly did."

"And he made sure everyone *saw* that tattoo, which would have been foolish if it was a real tattoo he couldn't remove," Jupiter emphasized. "I believe he is an ordinary man, younger and not swarthy, and with no tattoo! And I am convinced he must be the Amazing Gabbo. Only a trained carnival performer could fool Mr Carson."

"But there's no human fly in the show, Jupe," Pete said.

"No, he wouldn't use his real act. But most carnival performers can do other acts."

"And Andy said Mr Carson doesn't really know Gabbo," Bob pointed out.

"Exactly," Jupiter agreed. "Andy said Mr Carson might know Gabbo if he really looked closely for him. But Gabbo has been in prison, and quite a few years have passed. If Gabbo kept to himself and was rarely seen out of some costume, Mr Carson would never recognize him. Each performer has his own private trailer or truck. If he changed in his trailer, it would be easy to be seen mostly only in his costume."

"The crooked cats, Jupe," Peter said. "What does he want with them? Is the money in them?"

"No, Second," said Jupiter. "That would be totally impracticable. I would guess that something inside one cat shows where the $100,000 is. Or is something he must have to retrieve his loot. A small map, a key, a sign that identifies him, or a left-luggage ticket!"

"Something he hid in a crooked cat during that fire in San Mateo in case he was searched!" Bob decided.

"Wow," Pete cried, "that would sure explain it all."

"But," Bob wondered, "if he has what he wanted from the crooked cat, wouldn't he go after his loot right away, as the Chief thinks? Would he stay around here?"

"No, I think he would stay at the carnival, Records," Jupiter stated firmly. "He is actually safest there, if no one knows he's a member and what he really looks like. He doesn't suspect that anyone has guessed that he's there. He must know the police are looking for him now. And he must realize that if he left the carnival now he'd draw attention to himself. No, his best course now is to lie low! At least until the carnival leaves Rocky Beach, or closes."

"Well," Pete said, "if you're right, he won't do any more at the carnival. He isn't out to wreck it."

"Yes," Jupiter pronounced, "we can safely say there will be no more accidents. And the carnival will be open any minute now. It's time to catch our robber! We'll take our signallers, just in case. Come on, fellows."

They crawled out through Tunnel Two, and on their bikes rode towards the carnival. It was dusk, with the mountain wind rising strong. They parked their bikes near the carnival and joined the early crowd of customers streaming towards the entrance. Suddenly shouts rose ahead!

The people round them began to run towards the carnival.

"Something happened at the carnival!" Pete cried.

"It sounds like some accident!" Bob exclaimed.

Jupiter blinked as he began to run, too. "It can't be another accident! I know I'm right!"

15

The Robber Strikes!

THEY pushed through the gawking crowd and saw the carousel broken and tilted over on to the ground. Mr Carson was shouting orders to his crew of roughnecks.

The boys found Andy looking at the carousel in despair.

"What happened, Andy?" Pete asked.

"We don't know, Pete," the carnival boy replied in an agitated voice. "It was turning, ready for the first ride, when the engine started smoking, and it tilted over and collapsed! Three horses broke, see?"

Roughnecks were working feverishly with levers to raise the carousel back on a level. Others hammered the broken horses back together, and Mr Carson was trying to repair the smoking engine. He stood up to wipe his brow, and a knot of angry performers surrounded him.

"How many more accidents do we have, Carson?" Khan said.

"Your equipment is in bad repair," The Great Ivan said. "We are all uneasy."

"The equipment is fine," Mr Carson said. "You know that."

The tall, sad clown said, "Carousels don't break easily. It's a sign! We must close this unlucky show!"

"It *is* an unlucky show!" the fire eater said. "Maybe Rajah's escape was a third accident after all, and the next three are beginning!"

All the performers murmured, nodding their heads.

"We have to close, Mr Carson," a wire walker said.

"After tonight," the tall clown said. "Immediately!"

"How can you go on?" Khan asked. "How can you pay us all with no carousel, and—"

Mr Carson stood and looked at them all helplessly. The roughneck who had been working on the engine with him looked up and began to talk urgently to him. Mr Carson looked worried, but he faced the performers with a sudden smile.

"The carousel will be fixed and running within half an hour," he announced. "No real damage but a burned-out bearing. Now, let's get on with the show!"

"There will be worse, I know it," the tall, sad clown said.

But most of the performers began to smile again. They nodded with relief and hurried away to their tents and booths. Khan was the last to leave.

"The show is dangerous, Carson," the strong man said in a warning voice. "Too many mistakes and accidents. You should close."

Khan stalked away, and Mr Carson stared after him. Then he turned to the boys with troubled eyes. They could see that he was very worried. He had his whole future, and Andy's future, in the carnival.

"Are they going to work, Dad?" Andy asked.

"They'll work. Carnival people are happy folk. They forget trouble quickly—as long as we have no more accidents."

"The carousel's okay?" Andy hoped.

"Yes, Andy," Mr Carson said, his face grim. "That's not what worries me. My roughneck mechanic tells me that the bearing was tampered with, and the bolts were loosened, so that when the bearing froze the bolts were sure to shear. That's what knocked the carousel over."

"You mean it was sabotaged, Mr Carson?" Bob exclaimed.

"Yes, I do," Mr Carson said. "I owe you three boys an apology. It seems that someone must be trying to ruin the carnival."

Jupiter burst out, "Perhaps not, sir! I think a bank robber may be causing your troubles!"

"Bank robber?" Mr Carson said, staring. "You mean that robbery on our last night in San Mateo?"

"Yes, sir!" Jupiter declared. "I think the bank robber is a member of your carnival!"

Mr Carson flared up. "That's ridiculous, son! The police did come, and found no one!"

"Because he set off the fire in San Mateo, sir," Jupiter rushed on. "He set it to give him time to get out of his disguise, and to hide something in a crooked cat! That's why he was after the cats."

"No, Jupiter, none of our people look anything like the man the San Mateo police wanted. No one is tattooed."

Pete blurted out, "Jupe says he was in disguise all the time except here! Even the tattoo is a fake."

Mr Carson looked at them all. "Well, that is possible, I suppose, but who—"

Jupiter burst in, "I think I know who he is already, sir! From his escapes, some clothes we found, and what Andy told us, I'm certain the robber is the Amazing Gabbo!"

"Gabbo?" Mr Carson said, his face taking on a strange expression as he studied the boys.

"Yes, sir!" Jupiter continued. "Andy told us you don't really know him by sight. I think that if you—"

"No, Jupiter," Mr Carson stopped the First Investigator, his hand held up. "Boys, your logic and deductions are excellent. Very impressive, really. But you see, when the police told me of the robber's escape from that blind alley. I recalled Gabbo and his criminal record at once. I realized that he just might hide in a carnival, and that I wouldn't recognize him—unless I knew he was around and made a point of looking for him. So I did. I studied all of my performers—out of costume!"

Jupiter stammered, "You . . . you looked, sir?"

"I did, Jupiter," Mr Carson said in a kindly voice. None of them remotely resembles Gabbo. Most of them are much too old, anyway. No, if the robber was part of the carnival, it could explain the fire and Rajah's escape, but it doesn't explain the loss of our pony ride earlier, and what possible reason would the robber have for wrecking the carousel now?"

Jupiter was glum. "The carousel breaking is a disturbing development, sir," he admitted lamely.

"I'm sorry, but it looks more as if someone is trying to ruin my carnival—probably Andy's grandmother," Mr Carson said unhappily. "I agree that the man after those crooked cats must be the robber, but he must be an outsider and we won't see him again, I'm sure. From what you tell me, he has what he wanted. He would have no reason to wreck the carousel."

"Gosh," Pete said. "I guess not, Mr Carson."

"However, I'm asking you boys to keep an eye open and see if you can find who's causing these accidents. I have to get back to work, but you boys are free to go anywhere in the carnival. Just be careful."

"We will, Dad," Andy promised.

Mr Carson nodded thoughtfully, smiled at the boys, and went back to supervise the work on the carousel. The boys all looked at each other. Jupiter bit his lower lip.

"I was absolutely sure I was right," the First Investigator insisted.

"But Mr Carson is right, First," Bob said. "The robber wouldn't have any reason to wreck the carousel."

"He must be miles away by now," Andy added.

"Perhaps," Jupiter said. "But say he isn't, fellows. Say he's still here. There *are* two possible motives for him to wreck the carousel. He could be trying to close the show

90

so that he wouldn't be noticed when he left the carnival."

"He wouldn't try that so soon, would he, Jupe?" Andy asked. "I mean, he'd wait for things to calm down."

"I suppose he would," Jupiter agreed. "But, fellows, what if he hasn't yet found what he's after in those crooked cats? Are you certain you had only five cats, Andy?"

"I'm sure, Jupiter. I had five when we set up here."

"I wonder . . ." Jupiter mused. "Could whatever it is he wants have fallen out of the crooked cat? Maybe it wasn't in any of the cats. If so, it might be in your equipment trailer! Is your trailer at the shooting gallery now, Andy?"

"Of course, Jupe. You know I keep it there so I can keep an eye on it."

"But you're not watching it now, are you?" Jupiter exclaimed. "You're here because the carousel broke down!"

"You mean he's distracting us all again!" Pete cried.

"Why not? It worked twice before," Jupiter said. "The carousel damage is minor. If someone was trying to shut down the carnival, wouldn't they have tried to damage it more? Hurry, fellows, let's go to Andy's trailer!"

They walked quickly, but quietly, from the carousel to the shooting gallery. The crowd of customers had grown now, and the boys circled cautiously through them to the rear of the shooting gallery. The instant they rounded the back of the booth into the dark rear area, they saw dolls, toys, and other small prizes strewn over the ground.

"It's been broken open!" Andy whispered.

"Look!" Bob pointed.

A shadow seemed to flit from behind the trailer. The shadow of a man who ran in the night—across the open ground behind the carnival booths and tents, through a narrow hole in the temporary fence, and on towards the abandoned amusement park.

"After him!" said Jupiter.

91

16

A Chase in the Night

"There," Pete said quietly, "he's going through the fence!'

"Don't let him see us," Jupiter said.

They slipped through the fence one by one and stood in the dark, silent grounds of the old amusement park. The rickety roller coaster towered above them in the light of the rising moon. A strong mountain wind blowing out to sea made the old timbers creak and whine eerily.

"I don't see him," Bob said softly.

"Wait," Jupiter whispered. "Listen."

Crouched in the shadow of the high fence, they all listened in the night. The gay music from the repaired carousel sounded miles away outside the fence. Nothing moved in the darkness of the abandoned amusement park. To the left they heard the steady *lap-lap-lap* of water in the tunnel of love. There were small, scurrying sounds that could only be rats. They heard no other sounds in the ominous silence.

"He can't have gone far," Jupiter said in a low voice. "We'll split up, fellows. Pete and I will go to the right round the roller coaster. Bob and Andy will go left."

"You think it's the robber, Jupe?" Andy asked.

"I do," Jupiter said. "I think he did fail to find what he wanted in the cats, so he searched the trailer. If he found it in the trailer, he's going to be really dangerous now. If you see him, just follow him. Don't try to catch him."

They all nodded, and Bob and Andy vanished to the left towards the tunnel of love and the ocean side of the roller coaster, Jupiter and Pete moved quietly between the sagging roller coaster and the laughing mouth of the fun house.

The night made the abandoned rides and shows look like the landscape of the moon. Pete and Jupiter had passed the fun house, and were continuing on round the ghostly roller coaster, when Pete suddenly crouched down.

"Jupe! I hear something!" Pete whispered.

In the darkness under the beams of the roller coaster, and somewhere behind them now, they heard a small sound. It came again—a soft scraping like heavy shoes on rough wood. Then, what could only be quick footsteps running back away from them.

The heavy steps of a man.

"I see him!" Pete hissed to Jupiter. "He's going towards the fun house."

"Can you see who he is?"

"No," Pete said. "He's gone into the fun house!"

"Hurry, Pete. There might be another way out!"

They hurried silently across the moonlit open space to the gaping mouth of the fun house. Inside, they listened. They were in a dark passage that faded into blackness ahead. Shafts of silver moonlight through holes in the rotted roof were the only illumination.

"He had to go straight ahead, Jupe," Pete whispered.

As if to confirm Pete's statement, they heard a sharp, creaking noise in front of them, followed instantly by a thud and a sharp cry. Something heavy seemed to slide and bang against wood. The creaking sound came again, with another bang—and silence.

They looked at each other uneasily, and began to move cautiously forward along the dark, moonlit passage. Vaguely, they made out a closed door straight ahead.

"Be careful when you open—" Jupiter began.

The First Investigator got no farther in his warning about the door. With a sudden creaking noise the floor of the passage dropped away at a steep angle. They slipped flat on their backs, and slid wildly down the tilted floor as if on a playground slide.

There was nothing to hold on to. Flailing their arms, they slid down pell-mell until they hit with a thud against the wall ahead.

"Oooof!" The breath was knocked out of both of them.

Untangling their arms and legs, they sat up—and watched in dismay as the floor that had tilted down so suddenly creaked and groaned and swung up again, becoming the ceiling of the dark, narrow hole in which they sat!

"The whole floor tilted down!" Pete exclaimed. "It must be balanced so that when someone walks on it past the centre it drops like a see-saw."

"It's a fun house trick that still works," Jupiter realized. "The robber must have fallen down it ahead of us, but where did he go?"

"There's only one way," Pete said.

Directly in front of them was a narrow, round opening like a pipe. There was no other way out of the hole.

"Be careful," Jupiter whispered, "there might be a trick."

They crawled into the narrow tunnel. It was short, and they emerged into a room. Light filtered through wide cracks in the ceiling.

Except that it wasn't the ceiling above them—it was the floor!

"Juuuuupe!" Pete's voice quavered.

They seemed to be upside down in the dim, silvery room. The floor with its chairs, tables, and rug was above their heads. A ceiling light fixture stood straight up in front of them, and upside-down paintings floated in front of their startled eyes.

Jupiter whispered, "Another trick, Pete. They probably used lighting effects to make it better when they were operating."

"You're sure we're not upside down?" Pete said doubtfully.

"Of course I am," Jupiter insisted. "There's another round tunnel ahead leading out of here. Come on."

The new tunnel was much larger. As they stepped through, it moved and rocked. They realized that it had once been a revolving barrel. Though it no longer turned, it was still unsteady, and they stumbled through holding on to the rocking sides.

"Listen," Jupiter warned.

Somewhere ahead was a faint noise, like someone stepping very quietly.

"There," Pete whispered, and then gasped, "Oh—!"

They were in a longer and wider room than the other. It's ceiling was badly rotted, and bright moonlight filled it, casting deep, moving shadows. But it wasn't the shadows that had made Pete gulp.

Jupiter stared in fright.

A strange shape moved near the wall to the right. A monstrous apparition that looked straight at the boys. It was tall, horribly thin, with an enormous swollen head and arms as long and thin as tentacles. Its whole weird body seemed to flow and shift in the silver light like a giant, human snake.

"Wha . . . what . . . is it?" Pete stammered, moving close to Jupiter.

Jupiter gulped, "I don't know . . . I . . . ." and then began to laugh nervously. "It's mirrors, Pete! We're in the crazy hall of mirrors! We're seeing ourselves in twisted mirrors!"

"Mirrors?" Pete swallowed, "then why do I hear walking?"

"I don't hear—" Jupiter began.

"Oh, no! Is that a mirror!?" Pete wailed very low.

Directly ahead, away from the mirrors, a shape crouched in the dim moonlight as if listening, watching. A broad-shouldered shape, bare to the waist, with wild black hair and a black beard.

"Khan!" Pete cried louder than he had intended.

The strong man became alert. "Come out of there!"

Jupiter gripped Pete's arm. "He can't see us."

Khan growled. "I hear you! I've got you now!"

"That way!" Pete whispered. "A door!"

They slipped through the door Pete had seen among the mirrors. They found themselves in a narrow corridor with no ceiling. Ten feet inside it branched into two passages. Behind them, they heard a sharp oath as Khan found the door.

"Left, Jupe, that's the way out!" Pete urged.

The Second Investigator led them racing along the passages that branched every ten feet or so, always taking the left turn. Somewhere behind them Khan pounded along, banging into walls. The boys at last reached a door, tore it open, and came out—into the hall of mirrors again!

"It's a maze!" Jupiter realized in dismay. "Another fun house trick. We've gone in circles."

"Khan's coming behind us!" Pete groaned.

Jupiter chewed his lip. "There's always a key. That way got us nowhere. We'll go the other way each turn!"

They hurried back through the same door they had started with, and this time they took each right turn when the passages branched. For a time as they ran through the passages they heard Khan floundering behind them. Then his noises faded, and they reached a double door. They tumbled through it—and stood in the open between the side of the fun house and the entrance to the tunnel of love.

"It worked, Jupe!" Pete said.

"Yes, it did." Jupiter preened. "Now we'll find Mr Carson, and tell him that Khan—"

There was a sudden tearing crash of wood. As the two boys stared in fright, the massive figure of Khan smashed through a wall of the fun house, his eyes gleaming wildly!

17

A Black Shape

JUPITER AND PETE crouched low in the shadows, holding their breath as Khan stood listening where he had smashed through the wall of the Fun House.

"He doesn't see us yet," Jupiter whispered, his voice shaky, "but he will soon, Pete."

"We can't get to the fence," Pete said. "He's between us and the fence. But if we don't get out of here, he'll see—"

Jupiter whispered, "The tunnel of love! Crawl, Pete!"

The entrance to the tunnel of love was close, and they could crawl all the way to it in the shadow cast by the towering roller coaster. Water gleamed like black lead in the channel that vanished inside the covered building of the abandoned ride. The boys crawled into the entrance unseen by Khan and stood up some yards inside.

"I don't hear him following," Pete said.

"He didn't see us," Jupiter agreed. "He'll look soon, and he'll stay out there. He knows we're around, and he knows that we saw him. We'll have to find another way out of this tunnel."

They moved carefully along the edge of the sluggish

D

water of the channel. Deeper inside the building the path became a narrow, wooden catwalk. It was wet and slippery, intended only for emergency exit and for access to the platforms where startling objects had once jumped up to frighten the tunnel-of-love patrons. The platforms were empty now, and the only thing they saw as they walked was an old rowing boat tied to the catwalk.

"Jupe! I feel some wind," Pete said. "There must be an opening up ahead."

"Near the ocean, Pete. Be careful, Khan might know—"

They both heard the noise—a sharp creak of a loose board somewhere ahead of them!

It came again, as if someone was stepping softly between them and the opening ahead.

"Gosh, he must have gone round to cut us off!" Pete said.

"Don't move, Pete," Jupiter warned nervously.

They stood paralyzed on the narrow catwalk. Far ahead, in a patch of the moonlight through a hole in the roof, they saw something move.

"He's coming at us!" Pete whispered.

"Back the way we came! Hurry," Jupiter urged.

The ghostly figure ahead of them moved again, and both boys heard the unmistakable click of a pistol being cocked! Pete touched Jupiter.

"First!" Pete hissed. "If we go back we have to cross moonlight! He'll see us sure! He'll shoot!"

"The boat!" Jupiter said desperately.

The old rowing boat was tied up close to them. A heavy canvas tarpaulin covered the front end. Careful to make no sound, they slipped down into the boat and slid under the tarpaulin. They lay motionless in the dark, even trying not to breathe.

Minutes passed.

Then they heard soft steps on the catwalk above them. There was the faint squeak of soft rubber soles against

Together they pushed back the heavy tarpaulin . . .

wood, and a clink of metal against wood, as if the man's pistol had struck against a wall.

They heard nothing more.

Silence.

The boat rocked on the sluggish water of the narrow channel, and scraped against the wood of the catwalk.

The unseen man above them moved again, softly, his rubber soles squeaking directly over their heads for a time. The boat began to rock more, as if the unseen man had touched it. Then the rocking became gentler, lighter, with the sound of the man's soft shoes moving close alongside.

Under the canvas the boys could only wait, holding their breath. And after some more minutes, they no longer heard the shoes above them. They heard nothing but the *slap-slap* of water against the boat.

"He's gone!" Pete whispered.

Under the tarpaulin in the rocking boat, Jupiter didn't answer. Pete peered at his companion and saw dimly that the First Investigator was staring into empty space, his thoughts miles away.

"Pete," the stocky leader said suddenly, "we must get back to the carnival at once! I think I've solved the puzzle!"

"You mean Khan solved it by chasing us!"

"Yes, in a way he did," Jupiter said vaguely, still thinking. "I know where to find what that robber has been searching for!"

"You mean you don't think he has it?"

"No, I don't. I think we've all been looking in the wrong—"

The small boat gave a violent roll and lurch, and seemed to bounce wildly on the water. Jupiter held on, and Pete sat alert under the canvas.

Pete's head was cocked, listening. "Jupe, there's something funny! This boat's rocking too much! I don't hear

100

it scraping against the wood any more! What's happened? Open the canvas!"

Together, they pushed the heavy tarpaulin back and tried to stand up. Wind struck their faces, and the boat rocked so violently they fell back. Pete stared around.

"We're out on the ocean!" he cried.

The dark shape of the abandoned amusement park was far behind them already, and the lights of the carnival grew rapidly smaller. Jupiter looked at the boat's rope.

"It was cut, Pete! That old tunnel-of-love ride must be open to the ocean, and the robber knew it! He towed the boat out along the catwalk and set us adrift."

"The tide's going out, and the current's strong here on an outgoing tide!" Pete said. "We're drifting out fast."

"Then we'd better get back fast!"

Pete shook his head. "This boat doesn't have any oars, Jupe! No motor, no sails! We can't get back."

"We have to! We'll swim!" Jupiter cried.

The stocky leader dived over the side without another word. Pete followed, and both boys struck out for shore. But the current was too strong.

"I can't . . . do it, Pete," Jupiter gasped.

Pete was the more powerful swimmer, but even he struggled in the grip of the current. "We'll never make it! Back to the boat!"

They swam with the current and gradually caught the drifting boat. They clambered over the side and lay panting. Then Jupiter struggled up.

"The signaller!" he said. "Bob will see our signal!"

The First Investigator took the small instrument from his pocket and spoke urgently into it to start the signal. Then he stared at it in dismay.

"It won't work, Pete! The water ruined it!"

They began to yell for help, but their words were lost in the wind. Already they were too far from land to be heard, and no boats moved anywhere on the dark water.

The shore lights were distant points as the boat wallowed on the surging moonlit ocean. Water broke over the gunwales.

"Bail, Jupe," Pete ordered. "Those two cans are bailers!"

Jupiter bailed. "We must get back, Pete!"

"Not against this current!" Pete declared. "The wind is on-shore now, that'll slow us, but without oars or sails—"

Pete stopped. He stared at Jupiter. The stocky boy had ceased bailing, his hand suspended in mid-air as he looked straight ahead over Pete's shoulder. His hand moved to point shakily straight ahead.

"Pete! What's that big, black—"

Pete whirled in the boat to look.

Vague in the moonlight, directly ahead of the rocking boat, an enormous black shape seemed to rise out of the ocean and tower over them.

18

Marooned!

BOB AND ANDY had cautiously circled the opposite way round the old roller coaster and returned to where they had started—without meeting Pete and Jupiter. Bob looked round slowly.

"Andy, something's wrong," he said. "We should have met them, or found them back here."

"Look!"

The carnival boy pointed to the jagged hole in the fun house wall.

"That hole's new, Bob! I'm sure."

The two boys stared all round them in the gloom of the moonlit amusement park.

Bob called, "Pete! Jupe!"

"I hear someone coming!" Andy said.

They heard running outside the amusement park, and two men came through the hole in the fence.

"It's your Dad," Bob said to Andy.

Mr Carson ran up. "Are you boys all right?"

"We are," Bob said, "but we can't find Pete and Jupe."

Andy said, "We chased a man from my equipment trailer and split up in here, and now Pete and Jupiter are gone, Dad!"

Mr Carson frowned "Then Khan was right."

The bearded strong man walked up behind Mr Carson, his muscles and heavy boots shining in the moonlight. He nodded to the boys.

"I saw someone searching Andy's trailer," Khan explained. "I chased him in here, but lost him in the fun house."

Bob asked, "You didn't see Pete or Jupe?"

"No, boys. I didn't see them."

"All right, be calm," Mr Carson said, taking charge. "Andy, go and get a crew of roughnecks with lights. Khan, Bob, and I will start searching the grounds in the open."

Andy raced off, and Bob followed Mr Carson and Khan as they began to search the abandoned amusement park. They found no trace of Pete or Jupiter. Soon Andy came back with the crew of roughnecks. Carrying powerful electric lanterns, they spread out to search inside all the old buildings. Mr Carson and Khan went with the roughnecks, telling Bob and Andy to stay outside. Bob stood with puzzled eyes.

"Andy," he said, "Khan says he chased a man from your trailer. If he did, why didn't we see *two* men?"

"I don't know, Bob. We should have, I guess."

103

"I don't think there were two men! I think it was Khan we chased!"

"You mean," Andy gasped, "that Khan's the robber?"

Bob nodded. "Jupiter was suspicious of him all along. You don't even know his real name. He's been sneaking around. He's watched us. He's tried to convince your Dad to close the show. Now I think he's caught Pete and Jupe, and he's trying to lead us in the wrong direction! Let's find your Dad, quick!"

They hurried towards the fun house where lights flashed and bobbed through the cracks in the rotted walls. Just as they got to the entrance, Mr Carson came out, mopping his brow.

"No sign yet, boys," he said, "but we'll find them."

"I don't think you will, sir!" Bob declared hotly. "I think Khan is fooling us! He's the robber, and he knows where they are!"

"Khan?" Mr Carson said, his face serious. "That's a grave charge, Bob. What proof do you have?"

"I'm sure he was the only man at Andy's trailer. He was the man we chased. But he caught Pete and Jupe, and now he's leading us away from them. I know he is, sir!"

Mr Carson hesitated. "That's not exactly proof, Bob. And don't forget Khan is in charge of security at the carnival. He has a right to be poking around. But it's funny that your stories don't agree. Let's find Khan and ask him for more details."

Mr Carson went back into the fun house. The boys waited nervously outside. Ten minutes passed. Bob paced in the dark. What if he was wrong? He was sure, but if he—

Mr Carson came back walking quickly. His face was dark and grim. "Khan isn't in the fun house any more! No one has seen him. He told some of the roughnecks he had to go back to the carnival, but he never told me that! Come on, boys."

104

They hurried through the fence and back to the carnival grounds. Khan wasn't in his tent, or at his trailer. No one had seen him anywhere. And no one had seen Pete and Jupe.

"I think," Mr Carson said. "We'd better get the police."

Out on the ocean, where the giant black shape loomed high ahead of the bouncing boat, Pete gave a cry:

"It's Anapamu Island! It's the smallest of the channel islands. and closest to shore—less than a mile. Let's try to reach it!"

"I don't think we can miss it, Pete!" Jupiter pointed out. "We're drifting straight for it."

The boys held on to the gunwales of their wallowing craft as the small island loomed closer. They began to make out trees and rocks on the steep sides and a line of breakers.

"The beach is over there," Pete pointed to the left. "But there are rocks, Jupe! I think—"

Instead of finishing what he was going to say, Pete dived over the side and came up behind the boat. Grasping the stern of the boat and kicking, he steered it past the rocks and into the quiet waters of the sheltered beach.

Jupiter scrambled out, and together they ran the boat up on to the sand.

"We made it," Pete gasped.

"But we're marooned!" Jupiter cried. "How do we get off this island, Pete? We must get back to stop the robber!"

"Gosh, Jupe, it's just a small, deserted island—rocks and trees and an emergency shelter. I don't see how we can get back until tomorrow, at least. Boats pass in the day."

"Tomorrow could be too late," Jupiter insisted. "Come on, where's that emergency shelter?"

Pete led the way to a small cabin with a smaller shed.

The cabin contained nothing but a crude wooden table, some chairs and bunks, and a small stove and some food. The shed behind had two small boat masts, two booms, a small rudder with a long tiller handle, and piles of rope and boards. There were nails and tools, and that was all.

"There's no radio, Jupe," Pete said. "We're stuck until morning when we can hail a boat, or someone looks for us."

Jupiter didn't answer. He was looking at the contents of the shed.

"Pete, could we sail back in the boat if we had a sail?"

"Maybe—if we had a mast and a rudder."

"We have a mast and a rudder now, and that tarpaulin in the boat would make a sail!"

Pete was dubious. "Those masts are too big, Jupe, even if we had a way of stepping one in the boat."

"Stepping? What do you mean?"

"That's a nautical term for fixing a mast into a socket or supporting frame," said Pete. "You've got to hold the bottom of the mast in place somehow."

"Well, what about the booms? They're half as long. Could we step one of them?"

Pete pondered. "Yes, we could step it through a hole in a seat. There's a saw in the shed, and a hatchet. We could use boards to brace the boom at the bottom of the boat! Jupe, I think—oh, no, I forgot! We can't do it!"

"Why not?"

Pete stood glum. "The rowing boat doesn't have a keel. Not even a centreboard or sideboards. The boat would capsize in the wind. Even if we didn't capsize, without a keel we couldn't sail straight."

Jupiter sat down heavily. He chewed on his fingers, and stared at the useless booms and masts in the shed. He looked at the long masts.

"Pete?" he said. "Would those masts float?"

"I guess so. You want to ride home on a mast?"

Jupiter ignored Pete's humour. "What if we took some long boards and nailed them to the masts. Then we nail the other ends of the boards to the gunwales of the boat, and—"

"Outriggers!" Pete cried. "Jupe, it'll work! They won't be perfect, but we don't have more than a mile to sail! With the wind as it is, the outriggers will hold the boat up!"

"Hurry then, Pete! We must get back right away!"

19

A Strange Sight

OVER two hours had passed since Bob had first told his suspicious to Chief Reynolds. So far the police had found no trace of Jupiter, Pete or the missing Khan. Chief Reynolds paced just outside the entrance to the carnival. Inside, crowds of people were enjoying themselves, unaware of the drama around them. Mr Carson, Bob and Andy waited uneasily.

"Then you think this Khan is the bank robber, Bob?" Chief Reynolds asked again.

"Yes, sir!"

"I was beginning to wonder if the robber had really fled Rocky Beach. Too many people have claimed to have seen him, but no one actually has."

"That's just what Jupe said," Bob said.

"Jupiter is a bright lad," Chief Reynolds acknowledged.

"He thinks the robber is still after what he hid in the crooked cat," Bob said, "and I think Khan was searching

Andy's equipment trailer. That proves he's the robber! He was looking for what he had hidden."

"Yes, that could well be, boys," the Chief said.

"Khan is a strange man. He stayed aloof from us," Mr Carson said. "He never got friendly with anyone."

"Well, we'll find him," Chief Reynolds said grimly.

The police, and Mr Carson's roughnecks, had spread out over the entire area. They were searching the open lot, all the carnival booths and tents, and vehicles. No cars or trucks had been reported missing. They were combing the old amusement park again, and searching all along the edge of the ocean, and through the streets and buildings near the carnival. After still another hour they had found no trace of the boys or Khan.

"I'm worried," Chief Reynolds admitted at last. "They seem to have vanished into thin air. But we won't give up. I think that that old amusement park is the key, so I have men searching all through it again for—"

Shouts came suddenly from far off inside the amusement park.

"It's my men!" Chief Reynolds exclaimed. "They've found something! Follow me, boys!"

The boys and Mr Carson hurried after the Chief through the hole in the high fence. At the edge of the dark ocean they saw a knot of policemen and roughnecks.

"Have you found them? The boys?" Chief Reynolds demanded.

"No, Chief," a policeman said, "but we found him!"

The knot opened, and two policemen pushed Khan forward. The strong man shook them off like flies and glared.

"What the devil does this mean!" Khan demanded.

The bearded strong man's muscles gleamed in the hard yellow light of the electric lanterns.

"Tell us what you're doing here, Khan!" Mr Carson snapped.

108

"That's my business, Carson."

Bob couldn't hold himself back. "He's the robber! Make him tell what he's done to Jupe and Pete!"

"Robber?" Khan roared. "I'm not the robber, you fools! I chased him. I told you that."

"And what have you been doing for the last three hours while we looked for you?" Chief Reynolds wanted to know.

"I came back here to look for the robber on my own! I had a hunch that—"

"He's lying!" Bob cried hotly. "I'll bet even that beard is false!"

Before Khan could move, Chief Reynolds reached out and grabbed his beard. Khan hurled the Chief off—and the black beard came off in the Chief's hand! They all stared at Khan.

"All right," Khan said, "of course it's false." The strong man went on to pull off his sideburns and wild wig, revealing himself as a young man with close-cropped light hair. "We all wear costumes in the carnival. What's a strong man without a black beard?"

"But you never took off your beard and hair, Khan!" Mr Carson said. "You were hired wearing that beard and hair! You let us think that was your real appearance— even when the San Mateo police questioned us all!"

Khan waved his massive hand. "You know why, Carson. I'm used to working better shows than your two-bit carnival. I didn't want to be recognized and have my reputation ruined."

"I don't think he's even a strong man!" Andy cried. "Is he Gabbo, Dad?"

"No," Mr Carson said, looking closely. "He's not Gabbo."

"But he *is* lying!" Bob accused hotly.

Khan faced them all menacingly, his muscles bulging. "Am I, boy? Then—"

Khan was staring out towards the ocean. "What—?"

"Chief, look!" a policeman cried.

Everyone looked out at the ocean. On the moonlit water was a strange sight—a lopsided, half-collapsed outrigger boat sailing raggedly up to the shore with Pete and Jupiter on their feet and waving to them with broad grins.

"It's them!" Bob said.

"Pete, Jupe!" Andy shouted.

Jupiter and Pete beached their ungainly craft and came running up to rejoin their friends. In a matter of minutes they had told the whole story of their hours on the ocean and the island.

"You sailed back in *that*?" Chief Reynolds asked.

"Pete is an excellent sailor," Jupiter replied, "and we had to get back at once! I think I know where to find what the robber has been looking for! I don't think he's found it yet!"

"But we have the robber, Jupe!" Bob said. "It was Khan there all along, just as you suspected."

Jupiter looked at the strong man standing surrounded by policemen and glaring angrily at them all.

"No," Jupiter said. "Khan isn't the robber."

Khan growled, "I told them that, boy."

"He's an impostor, Jupiter," Mr Carson said, "and he was searching Andy's trailer. You saw him!"

"No, sir, I don't think he was," Jupiter said politely but firmly. "When Pete and I were under the tarpaulin in that boat, I realized that there must have been *two* men, and that Khan was chasing the real robber. When he heard us in the fun house, he thought *we* were the robber."

"How do you deduce that, Jupiter?" Chief Reynolds asked.

"He warned us that he saw us, Chief," Jupiter said. "That is how a pursuer acts, not someone being pursued. The real robber would have wanted to remain hidden from us!"

The chief nodded, "Well, yes, I see. But you can't—"

"Also," Jupiter went on boldly, "Khan was bare to the waist when we saw him, and wearing only those tights. His hands were empty. He had no place to carry a pistol or a knife, and the man who set us adrift had both a pistol and a knife!"

"The boy is smarter than any of you," Khan declared.

"Finally," Jupiter added, "in the boat we distinctly heard the sound of soft, rubber-soled shoes on the man who cut us loose. You can all see that Khan is wearing his heavy boots."

Khan laughed. "I told you I was in the clear."

"Well, Mr Khan, I wouldn't say that," Jupiter pronounced. "I believe you are an impostor, and you are up to something you don't want known! You are in the carnival for some devious purpose. I expect Chief Reynolds can find out if he asks the right questions in the right place."

The First Investigator was looking at Khan with a cool smile. The strong man glanced round, and then looked straight back at Jupiter. At last he sighed.

"I guess you are a smart boy at that," Khan said. "All right. Yes, I'm here for a secret purpose. I'm a real strong man, but I retired a few years ago to become a private detective. My real name is Paul Harney, and Andy's grandmother hired me to keep an eye on Andy and the show. She honestly believes that carnival life is wrong for Andy. She sent me to protect him and to see how dangerous the show is."

"You didn't cause our accidents?" Mr Carson demanded.

"No, but when they began to happen I became worried. I did try to persuade you to close the show, Carson. I snooped around because the accidents seemed to endanger Andy, and I wanted to be sure they were just accidents."

"You were protecting Andy?" Mr Carson said.

"Yes, Carson. That was my job," Khan replied.

Jupiter frowned. "Most commendable. Mr Khan, or Harney, but I don't think it's the whole truth. You were at Andy's equipment trailer because you suspected that what the robber wanted might be in the trailer. You weren't protecting Andy!"

Khan's eyes glittered. He was silent for a moment. Then he nodded. "You're right, son. After the police questioned us all in San Mateo, I had a hunch that the bank robber was a member of the carnival. I'm a detective, and it would help my reputation if I caught a bank robber by myself. So I began to investigate. After Andy's cat was stolen, I guessed that the robber had put something in those crooked cats. But no one in the show fits the robber's description, and by now he has what he wanted. It wasn't in one of those cats after all."

"Jiminy," Andy said. "I guess it fell out of the cat."

Everyone else nodded glumly. All except Jupiter.

"On the contrary, fellows," the First Investigator declared. "What the robber wanted *was* in a crooked cat, and I believe that it still *is* in a crooked cat!"

20

Jupiter Deduces an Answer

"But, Jupiter," Andy protested, "I only had five crooked cats, and the robber found them all!"

"No, Andy, you had six cats," Jupiter declared triumphantly. "You had five you gave out here, but you have a sixth crooked cat—and we all saw it!"

Pete gaped. "We did, Jupe?"

"Where, First?" Bob demanded.

"Right before our eyes the first night," Jupiter said dramatically. "So obvious we overlooked it. You recall that first night in Andy's truck when Andy showed us his broken—"

Andy cried, "My broken prizes! In my work-basket! There *is* a crooked cat. It was burned in the San Mateo fire!"

"So it was in the shooting gallery the night of the fire," Jupiter said. "The robber hid whatever it is in that crooked cat, but it was damaged by the fire, and Andy took it away to repair. The robber never thought of that! But in the boat I realized that if the robber was still trying to get Pete and me out of the way, he *still* didn't have what he wanted even after searching Andy's trailer. I reasoned that there had to be a sixth crooked cat—and then I remembered Andy's work-basket!"

"Wow," Pete exclaimed in awe. "We'd never have thought of that, First."

"I never did, and I had the cat!" Andy said.

"It looks like the robber didn't think of it, either boys," Chief Reynolds said with a smile. "Fine work, Jupiter! I'm proud to have you as a junior assistant deputy."

Jupiter grinned proudly. "Well, sir, it was only logical once I realized—"

The First Investigator's words trailed off, and his head came up alertly. He looked round in the dark night.

"Chief! Someone is running away from here!"

Then they all heard it—someone runing fast, back towards the amusement park fence. The crowd of police and roughnecks all turned to look.

"Who is that running away?" Chief Reynolds demanded.

"I don't know, sir. We're all here," a policeman said.

"Some man, he was standing here I think," a roughneck said. "I didn't notice who he was."

"Did anyone notice a stranger?" Mr Carson asked.

Everyone shook his head. Then Bob exclaimed:

"Where's Khan!"

The strong man was nowhere to be seen!

"Quick, everyone," Jupiter suddenly cried. "Whoever it is heard all about the sixth cat! Hurry, Chief!"

They all ran across the abandoned amusement park and through the hole in the fence. As the last customers stared at them, they dashed through the carnival to where the trucks and wagons stood. Andy dashed inside his trailer. He came back out almost at once.

"The crooked cat, it's gone! He got it!"

Chief Reynolds cried, "Block all exits!"

"Search the grounds!" Mr Carson ordered his rough-necks.

The police and roughnecks went into action.

"He's got the crooked cat," Chief Reynolds declared, "but he won't get out with it! We're too close behind him."

"Chief?" Pete asked. "Could it be Khan?"

"Was he lying all the time, after all?" Mr Carson wondered.

"I don't know. He's a slick talker," the Chief said.

"Maybe he was hired by Grandma," Andy said, "but is the bank robber, too."

"I've known detectives to go wrong," Chief Reynolds said grimly. "But if he has, this time we'll get him. We're too close for him to have time to examine the cat and dispose of it. He'll have to try to leave the grounds, and we know what he looks like now."

"What if it isn't Khan, sir?" Pete asked. "We won't know who it is then, and he can hide the cat and just wait."

"No, Pete," Chief Reynolds shook his head. "This carnival isn't that big. We'd find the crooked cat—and him. Sooner or later he must try to escape now, and we'll have

114

him. He can't possibly get out with that cat. Jupiter I think—"

The Chief turned to find the First Investigator, Jupiter was nowhere around!

"Jupe!" Pete called.

"Jupiter? Where are you?" Chief Reynolds shouted.

There was no answer.

"I don't remember seeing him with us at all!" Bob said.

"Not since we left the old amusement park," Mr Carson said.

"Well, he can't be far," said Chief Reynolds.

Pete said shakily, "Unless he saw the robber and followed him!"

"Now be calm, Pete," Mr Carson said.

They all searched through the trucks and trailers, and then returned to the carnival grounds. After some fifteen minutes they met on one of the wide pathways near Andy's shooting gallery. They had not found Jupiter.

"The shows are over," Mr Carson said. "I'll ask all the performers if they've seen Jupiter."

"The exits are all blocked, and the fence is being watched," Chief Reynolds said. "He can't have left the grounds."

The performers were all gathered near The Great Ivan's show tent. They stood in an uneasy group, watching the police and roughnecks still searching and guarding the fence and exits. None of them remembered seeing Jupiter when Mr Carson asked them.

"I have seen nothing," The Great Ivan said uneasily.

The wire walkers and the fire eater shook their heads. The small, fat clown danced round awkwardly, still half performing his routine, and pointing at the tall, sad clown. The tall clown swept at the ground with his broom and dustpan with a broken bottom.

"Maybe I saw him," the tall clown said in his slow, sad voice. "Behind the tents with someone."

"You did?" Chief Reynolds snapped. "With whom?"

The tall clown shook his head. "I don't know."

The small clown did a ludicrous handstand that failed badly, and then began to jump up and down beside the tall clown. Bob groaned.

"The robber's got Jupe!" Bob cried. "I know it!"

"He'll use Jupe as a hostage to get away!" Pete moaned.

"Easy, boys," Chief Reynolds said, but his face was worried. "It does change matters. If he has Jupe, we'll have to let him go. But we'll know him, then, and we'll get him!"

Andy said, "If he has Jupiter, why hasn't he tried to use him as a hostage yet?"

"I don't know, Andy," Chief Reynolds admitted.

The tall clown suddenly said, "Hostage, Chief? When I saw that boy, the man with him was making towards a break in our fence that leads to the ocean!"

Chief Reynolds whirled. "What? The ocean?"

"He's trying to escape by swimming round the amusement park fence where you don't have a guard," Mr Carson cried.

Pete and Andy started to run towards the fence with the Chief and Mr Carson. But Bob didn't move. He stood staring at the dirt of the carnival pathway.

"Chief! Fellows," Bob said slowly. "Look at the dirt."

They all stopped and looked where Bob pointed. The small clown, still fooling around, was rolling on the ground and pointing up at the tall clown.

Near him, drawn in the dirt, was a large question mark!

21

A Robber Unmasked !

"OUR QUESTION-MARK SIGN!" Pete cried, and stared at the small clown who was still jumping round his tall partner.

"It's Jupe!" Bob realized. "He's telling us that—"

Before anyone could say anything more, the tall clown suddenly whipped a pistol from his floppy sleeve. He aimed the gun at them all. Without a word he began to back away towards the main entrance, his dark eyes glittering menacingly in his chalk-white clown's face.

"Don't move, anyone," Chief Reynolds warned. "Let him go."

Helpless, the boys, the Chief and Mr Carson watched as the clown backed farther and farther away. He was almost at the main exit from the carnival when a massive-figure jumped out from behind the Ferris-wheel booth. He was on the clown before anyone knew what was happening.

It was Khan. The tall clown tried to turn his pistol on the strong man, but Khan's hand clamped on his wrist and the pistol fell to the ground. The tall clown stood helpless in the grip of the strong man.

"So, one robber caught!" Khan said in triumph.

Chief Reynolds shouted for his men, and they came running to take the tall clown from Khan. Other policemen began to disperse the crowd of performers and late customers. Khan grinned.

"I was just watching and waiting for the robber to

make some move," the strong man explained. "But I must admit I never suspected the clown."

The small, fat clown peeled off his mask and putty nose to reveal a smiling Jupiter.

"I always wanted to be a clown," Jupe said.

Chief Reynolds said, "You better explain all this, Jupiter. How did you know the tall clown was the robber, and what are you doing in that costume?"

"Well," the First Investigator began, "when we began to chase that unseen man from the amusement park, I realized that he would get the crooked cat before we could. So instead of going with you all, I decided to go straight to the performing tents. I reasoned that after the robber got the crooked cat from Andy's truck, he'd run to where he could hide it, and himself, among a lot of people.

"I'd just reached the main show area, where there were still customers all around, when I saw the tall clown running right at me! I could see he was hiding something under his baggy jacket. If he saw me, he'd know I had guessed what he had and who he was! So I ducked into the first tent. That's when I got a real shock—it was the clown tent!"

"Wow!" Pete exclaimed. "You mean you were in the tent where he would come in for sure, First!"

Jupiter nodded. "An error of panic, I'm afraid, Second. I had to think quickly. The tent was in two parts, like all the show tents—the rear for resting between acts and dressing if the performer didn't dress in his own trailer. So I ran into the dressing section. I heard him come into the show part of the tent. He was busy out there for a few minutes. I didn't know if he'd come into the dressing section or not. I could see he didn't dress in the tent, only he might come back any minute!"

"Jiminy, you were trapped, Jupe," Andy said.

"I was, but I saw the costumes of the small clown! He dressed in the tent, and he'd already quit for the night and gone. So I got into his costume and mask. They fitted me just right! I'd just finished putting on the putty nose when he came back into the dressing section—he'd heard me, I guess. He thought I was the small clown, and he insisted we do one more act in the main alley!

"I realized, of course, that he wanted to do another act to have a chance to escape from the carnival with the crooked cat. The whole situation had changed for him, you see. All along he'd been trying to get the crooked cat without anyone knowing what he wanted. But now we all knew what he was doing, and hiding didn't matter any more. He just wanted to escape."

Chief Reynolds nodded. "I see that, Jupiter, but when you were in the open, why didn't you just tell us who he was?"

"I knew he had a pistol, sir," Jupiter said simply. "I was afraid if I revealed myself he'd start shooting. I had to get your attention *before* he learned I wasn't the small clown. So I drew the question mark in the dirt. Luckily, Bob saw it, and you were all alert before he realized I had accused him!"

"Not quite alert enough, he almost got away," the Chief said. "Fine work. Jupiter! Where it that crooked cat?"

"Strapped to his leg inside the baggy pants," Jupiter said.

One of the Chief's men searched the tall clown, and pulled out the crooked cat. He gave it to the Chief who quickly examined it, and held up a small piece of tan cardboard.

"A left-luggage ticket!" the Chief exclaimed. "He deposited the robbery money. That solves one part of the case. Now let's find out just who this robber is."

"Robber?" Mr Carson frowned. "But, Chief, he can't be—"

Before Mr Carson could finish what he was saying, Chief Reynolds had the tall clown's mask and wig off, and was wiping the make-up away. The Chief stepped back, his face incredulous!

Out of his clown face, the tall clown was a thin, white-haired old man! At least sixty-five years old!

"Bu-but—" The Chief stammered. "He can't be the robber!"

"I was trying to tell you," Mr Carson said. "He's too old for the robber. He couldn't disguise his age that well, and he could never climb walls like the robber."

"No . . . he couldn't," Jupiter said slowly, dismayed.

The old clown looked at the ground. "I . . . I was hired. I admit I took that crooked cat. He said he'd pay me ten thousand dollars! He gave me the gun, but I don't even know how to use it. I'm sorry I threatened you. I was afraid."

"Who hired you?" Chief Reynolds demanded.

The old clown looked round. "Him! Khan! He hired me."

The strong man grew red. "He's lying! I told you—"

"I'm telling the truth," the old clown insisted. "Don't take my word, Chief. Take us both to jail, and then check on Khan. I know I've got punishment coming, but Khan hired me."

For a moment everyone stood staring at both the old clown and Khan. The clown's arm was pointing at Khan, and Jupiter was staring hard at both the clown and Khan. Then the First Investigator's eyes gleamed.

"One of them is lying, Chief," he said, "and I know that it's the old clown!"

Chief Reynolds demanded, "How do you know that, Jupiter?"

"The clown isn't an old man at all," Jupiter declared. "He's disguised in *reverse*!"

"Huh?" Pete exclaimed.

"Yes, Second," Jupiter insisted. "We're been looking

120

for a man who disguised himself as the swarthy tattooed man to rob the bank and fool us—for someone who *put on* a disguise. But he didn't do that. No, he's been disguised all along as the old man clown! To rob the bank, and buy the cats, he *took off* his disguise! Under that old man's face is our real robber!"

The old clown began to struggle, but the police held him firmly. Chief Reynolds felt the clown's face, pulled at the white hair, dug at the wrinkled skin.

"Jupiter! I can't get anything off his face!" he said.

"Modern disguise is very clever," Jupiter said. "Look all the way down on his neck."

The Chief pulled down the collar of the clown costume. They all saw a faint line round the clown's neck. Chief Reynolds dug his fingernails under it, tugged hard upward —and the old man's whole face, hair and neck skin came off in one piece of solid plastic!

The clown stood revealed as a swarthy, dark eyed man— just as he had looked when he had bought the crooked cats.

"It's him, the tattooed man!" Pete cried. "Without his tattoo!"

Mr Carson peered at the glaring robber. "And he *is* The Amazing Gabbo, too! He's changed, but it's Gabbo. So, you're a bank robber now, Gabbo?"

The robber snarled, "Go to the devil, Carson! All of you! I'd have got away except for those stupid kids!"

"Kids, Mr Gabbo," Chief Reynolds said grimly, "but not stupid. Take him and lock him up, men!"

As the glaring Gabbo was led away, Chief Reynolds turned to face Jupiter once more.

"All right, Jupiter, he had us fooled to the end," the Chief said. "That disguise was so perfect he might have escaped after all. You noticed how he wanted us to take him to jail with Khan? If he'd had a moment alone, even in jail, he would have stripped off that disguise, and perhaps walked away! How did you know it was a double disguise?"

"Well, sir, his plastic face was perfect," Jupiter said proudly, "but he forgot to disguise his hands! His hands were smooth, firm, dark and without wrinkles or age spots —young hands, Chief."

"By George," Chief Reynolds said, "you're right again!"

Bob and Pete both groaned aloud.

"He always is, sir," Bob said in mock despair.

"Most of the time, anyway," Pete said.

Jupiter only beamed in triumph.

22

A Report to Alfred Hitchcock

THE NEXT DAY, after Bob had written up the report of the case, the boys took it to their friend and mentor Alfred Hitchcock. The famous director read it, and immediately agreed to introduce the case for the boys once more.

"The Secret of the Crooked Cat," the great movie director intoned. "A most intriguing title for a most satisfactory exercise in gimlet-eyed observation and skilful deduction! You have all done well to end the nefarious career of The Amazing Gabbo before he could do more damage, boys!"

"He turned out to be wanted in the state of Ohio for an earlier robbery, sir," Bob said.

"That was one reason he joined the carnival in disguise," Jupiter explained. "He heard that Mr Carson was taking the show to California. To escape any detection, he assumed his old clown's disguise from the first. Later, he had the idea of robbing the San Mateo bank as *himself*, but with the fake tattoo to distract witnesses."

"Most ingenious," Mr Hitchcock commented thoughtfully. "I presume he then deposited his loot in that left-luggage room, and planned to slip back into the carnival, and simply leave town as the old clown—totally unsuspected as the younger robber!"

"Yes, sir," Jupiter agreed. "But when he was discovered accidentally at the carnival, he set off the fire to have time to hide the left-luggage ticket and get back into his old man's disguise. Only he failed in his haste to count the crooked cats. He didn't realize that there were six until he heard me tell Chief Reynolds what I had deduced."

Mr Hitchcock nodded. "He moved too carefully at first, as you deduced, Jupiter, and became too desperate later. The typical criminal mind, not very smart after all. I imagine he will pay for his errors in a California prison, eh?"

"And after that Ohio wants him!" Pete said. "He won't be performing his human fly act for a long time."

"No!" Mr Hitchcock mused, "unless there is a prison carnival! An idea that has great merit, boys. It might teach your foolish Gabbo to use his skills more wisely."

"Perhaps you should suggest that to the prison authorities, sir," Jupiter said with a grin.

"Me? Well, perhaps, young man," Mr Hitchcock said hastily. "But what of young Andy Carson's grandmother? Will she, too, mend her opinions of Mr Carson and carnivals?"

"She already has, sir," Bob said. "Khan, I mean Paul Harney, reported to her that the carnival is a good life for Andy, and quite safe."

"She is at least resigned to agreeing that a boy is best with his Dad," Jupiter added.

"Mr Harney liked being a strong man again so much," Pete said, "that he's staying with the carnival instead of going back to being a plain detective."

"Ah, is he?" Mr Hitchcock smiled. "I wonder if his decision may have been influenced by the demonstration of true detective skill by you boys, eh?"

Jupiter grinned. "Well, sir, I couldn't say."

"No, it will remain Khan's secret, I expect," the famous director said. "One point, my young friends. How did the loss of the carnival pony ride fit into the affair?"

"It was just a real accident after all," Bob explained.

"The piece that didn't fit, of course," Mr Hitchcock nodded. "So that ends your adventure with the carnival?"

"Well, almost," Jupiter said.

Pete blurted out, "Jupe's going to be a clown for a couple of days! Mr Carson is letting him take Gabbo's place for the rest of the performances in Rocky Beach."

"Bravo, Jupiter!" Mr Hitchcock cried. "Perhaps I shall come to see you perform."

With that, the boys trooped out of the famous director's office. Left alone, Mr Hitchcock smiled at the thought of Jupiter as a clown and wondered what the boys would come up with next.

says...

'Yo-ho-ho for your next book from the Armada ship! There's a cargo of exciting reading for you—so set sail with another Armada book now.

You'll find more titles listed over the page.'

Armada Science Fiction

Step into the strange world of Tomorrow with Armada's exciting science fiction series.

ARMADA SCI-FI 1
ARMADA SCI-FI 2
ARMADA SCI-FI 3

Edited by Richard Davis

Three spinechilling collections of thrilling tales of fantasy and adventure, specially written for Armada readers.

Read about . . . The monstrous Aliens at the bottom of the garden . . . A jungle planet inhabited by huge jellies . . . A robot with a human heart . . . The terrible, terrifying Trodes . . . A mad scientist and his captive space creatures . . . The deadly rainbow stones of Lapida . . . The last tyrannosaur on earth . . . and many more.
Stories to thrill you, stories to amuse you—and stories to give you those sneaking shivers of doubt . . .

Begin your sci-fi library soon!

Armada

THE FIRST ARMADA MONSTER BOOK

Edited by R. Chetwynd-Hayes

Meet twelve of the most fearsome creatures ever to have menaced the earth—or slithered out of the sea—in a bumper collection of monster stories in a new Armada series.

Monsters like Dimblebee's Dinosaur, frozen for centuries ... The Sad Vampire, who didn't like blood ... The terrible three-headed Chimaera ... The awful underwater menace at Hell's Mouth ... The shapeless black creature in the cellar ... The appalling Thing in the Pond ... Big-Feet: forty feet from snout to tail, with flapping ears and red, glaring eyes—and ticklish toes ... and lots more.

Also available

THE SECOND ARMADA MONSTER BOOK

Armada

CAPTAIN ARMADA

has a whole shipload of exciting books for you